BUSTER CALLAN

Other books by Brian McNaughton

Fiction

The Throne of Bones
Downward to Darkness
Worse Things Waiting
Gemini Rising
The House Across the Way
Nasty Stories
Even More Nasty Stories

BUSTER CALLAN

Brian McNaughton

WILDSIDE PRESS
Doylestown, Pennsylvania

Buster Callan
A publication of
Wildside Press
P.O. Box 301
Holicong, PA 18928-0301
www.wildsidepress.com

FIRST EDITION

For JOE CITRO, *who gave me some encouragement*
when I badly needed it, and who claimed to find
a grain of truth in my depiction of his beloved Vermont.

Chapter One

Trooper was one mean bastard of a dog. His full name, which Buster Callan had shortened for convenience, was Storm Trooper. He was German, after all, and he had a black-and-tan coat, but Buster had never supposed that the ballsy pup would grow up with a temperament to match his name. He hated all humans and feared none of them, but he respected Buster. That was all Buster asked.

Ace was different. He liked people and would clown around for them, but he loved Buster. Ace was the only creature that Buster had ever loved, with the exception of his mother, and he had stopped loving her when he was nine or ten years old and able to look at her objectively.

Ace, the black Labrador, romped ahead, but not too far. Whenever he seemed to be getting carried away with exuberance, Buster would call him back with a snap of his fingers. The forest sang with the skeletal clatter of loose birch bark, but Ace never failed to hear that one short snap and respond. Trooper stayed at Buster's side, where he had damned well better stay if he knew what was good for him, the cleft wedge of his monster skull on a line with his master's hip. His head was high, and his forepaws spurned the earth with circular strokes.

The dogs knew why they were out. They had both been bathed, and they were smart enough – Ace was, anyway – to know what that meant. Buster had bathed, too. He'd washed his clothes twice, then boiled them. Satisfied that they were as clean and as odorless as they could possibly be, he had rubbed them thoroughly with cow dung. That was a trick that Ace had always known – probably without knowing, at first, why he knew it. Whenever he got a bath, he would promptly run off to wallow in the smelliest mess he could find, anything that would mask the residual odor of dog. Some of those bow-and-arrow fairies who came up in their Robin Hood outfits had the same idea, smearing themselves with fancy concoctions of animal musk, but Buster didn't have that kind of money to throw away, and cowshit worked just fine.

Buster breathed deeply, filling his lungs with the crisp air of the May morning. He had grown accustomed to the smell of his clothes and his dogs, an odor that he had never found distasteful anyway. Automobile exhaust, though, could nauseate him. He still believed that was the main reason why the Army had been so uncongenial: the assholes had stuck him in a motor pool. Thinking of the trips he had made through the industrial hell of northern New Jersey, on his way to or from Fort Dix, he could almost taste the vomit in his throat again.

Never mind New Jersey, nowadays even Brattleboro or Bennington could make him sick. Too many people, too many cars, and too goddamned many out-of-state license plates. He had to laugh. He himself had gone across the river to New Hampshire to register his car, just so he could get plates that said LIVE FREE OR DIE. Which, it now occurred to him, was a double-edged motto, one that might just as well serve as a slogan for all the black brood-sow welfare chiselers in New York City.

The joy of the morning had lost some of its edge. The air seemed less crisp. Buster felt a knot forming under his heart. The New York City bankers had stolen the mills, spiriting them away to the cheap labor of the south, and thus had beggared the state. Then, no longer able to live in the mongrelized cesspool they'd made of their own city, they had come up here to rape the beggar, buying up the farms that had been abandoned because of their manipulations on Wall Street. Seeing rural mailboxes bearing names like Rosenfield and Stern, names unknown to his youth, caused him pain – actual physical pain.

Trooper broke away and ran ahead. Buster blamed himself. He believed – it was a belief he would have shared with no one – that his control of the dogs depended on a telepathic bond. By letting his mind stray to the thoughts that could gnaw at him like rats, that could distract him totally from the business at hand, he had lost his hold on Trooper. The shepherd bounced ahead on steel-sprung legs, tail up like a battle flag, big balls bouncing. Even in his anger, Buster could admire him as one hell of a dog.

He couldn't call out. Trooper had broken because of a scent, and any deer that he could smell would be able to hear Buster's command. The day was a waste, just like the last two days when he'd taken Trooper out. The dumb bastard just didn't have the subtlety required for this kind of work.

He knew what Ace could do to save the day, and Ace did it, reinforcing his master's belief in that telepathic bond. Trooper let out a "whuff" of shock as the black dog hit him high on the shoulder, knocking him ass over heels. Buster was on top of them, gripping Trooper in a headlock, before the shepherd could retaliate.

"Sit, you son-of-a-bitch!" Buster hissed.

Trooper's black lips stretched back from a set of white teeth that could have cracked Buster's thigh. Buster could feel as well as hear the rumble deep in the dog's barrel chest. He repeated his command and Ace took a stiff step forward. Trooper sat.

"Shit, I don't know," Buster said to Ace. "We oughtta chain up this son-of-a-bitch and go on by ourselves. It's got to the point, I'll level with you, where we just don't eat today if we don't luck out."

Head cocked, Ace listened, and with an expression of greater intelligence, Buster thought, than any of the people he ever talked to. Trooper, his rage forgotten, panted in the headlock that had become a companionable embrace, his tongue hanging ludicrously far out of his mouth.

"But look, Trooper, you gotta learn sometime, baby. I'm damned if I'll feel like going out tonight with a shotgun, which is what I'll have to do if you screw up again. Okay, you get one more chance. But I swear to Christ, I'll sell you to some tourist if you fuck us again. Heel, Trooper!"

Goddamned if he couldn't have been on parade at the Westminster Kennel Club, the worthless bastard. Ace, too, was on his best behavior, trotting at Buster's left in line with Trooper on his right. Perhaps the deer had heard their quarrel and the live scent was gone, and that's why they were acting like a couple of Park Avenue poodles out for an airing.

But the deer were there, alarmingly close, when the woods thinned and Buster got a clear view of the ski run sloping upward. He froze, a hand lightly on the neck of each dog. The dogs froze, too.

The ski runs were one product of the outsprawling cityswarm that Buster could live with. Deserted in the snowless months, they opened up the woods and gave the deer pasturage. Go there at night with a strong spotlight to blind and freeze the deer, as well as a shotgun to shorten the odds, and you had meat on the table. But there was no fun in that.

Eight does grazed while the stag, a tough old customer with a broken rack, tested the breeze. Buster seldom killed bucks, but he would have been tempted by this one if his antlers had been intact. He had to remind himself that he wasn't some pussy sportsman who killed for trophies.

The buck was edgy. No question about it, he'd heard something, or sensed something to key him up to a more than normal pitch of alertness. He kept chivvying the does into a tighter pattern than they wanted to maintain.

Buster waited, as still as the tintype of his great grandfather on the mantel at home. He felt a controlling bond flowing through him, through the dogs, through the deer. He could will the situation to develop as he wanted it, just as he could will his eyelids not to twitch and will his heart to beat less strongly.

A dappling cloud-shadow raced over the ski run. It seemed a signal for the buck to relax, for the herd to spread. Their general drift was uphill, away from Buster and his dogs. The stag lowered his head to browse among the young clover and the fiddleheads. Buster permitted himself to breathe again.

He flicked Trooper's muzzle with his fingertips. Tail down, ears high, the shepherd slithered downhill through the woods, disappearing with the silent speed of a snake. Buster and Ace studied each other for a moment. The equivalent of a shrug passed between them. Buster made a short motion with his hand, and the Labrador went uphill through the woods.

Once more Buster achieved a total calm that linked him with the animals. He cropped clover with the deer. He crept through the woods with the dogs. An element in this network, no more or less important than the dogs or the deer, clasped the worn handle of a bowie knife.

The center of the browsing herd had moved far uphill, two hundred yards or more. Fifty yards above them, Ace broke out of the woods, laughing and wagging his tail. Deer heads shot up, froze for a split second, but they didn't accept his invitation to play. They wheeled and bolted down the ski run. Ace ran flat out, but they steadily gained on him.

They stormed past Buster's spot. Wild eyes rolled, seeing him for the first time in passing. Fucking Trooper . . . but the shepherd made his move at the last possible moment; charging, roaring, slavering in the path of the deer. The herd rolled back on itself and exploded in all directions. Most of them bolted for the woods opposite Buster. Two dashed past him at wide angles. A confused doe tried to go three ways at once, tangling her legs, and stumbled. Trooper hit her from the right, hamstringing her with one flash of his ripping teeth, one furious shake of his big head. Ace hit her seconds later. Last of all Buster reached her, slicing through her jugular with one stroke, drenching his arm in hot blood.

Ace sat back and grinned. Buster sucked in deep breaths, letting them out as whoops of exultation. Trooper continued to rip chunks from the twitching doe's haunch, inhaling them, and it was a moment before Buster saw what the dog was doing.

"Hey, Trooper! No!"

The dog's yellow eyes fixed on Buster, but he continued to worry the doe's torn haunch.

"No, you son-of-a-bitch, get *back!*" Buster roared, moving forward with clenched fists.

The dog half rose, tail straight out, all his big teeth showing, and growled. Buster could see that he meant business. He kept his eyes locked on Trooper's in an answer to his challenge, but the periphery of his vision was busy. He saw a big stick. He bent and reached for it. Trooper sprang, roaring.

"Shit!" Buster spat, realizing it was a dead birch limb that he'd picked up. He swung it nevertheless, and it deflected the shepherd's charge even though it broke apart because of its inner rot.

Before he could recover from his swing and turn to face the dog directly, Trooper was on him. Buster hit the ground full-length under the weight of the hundred-and-fifty pound shepherd. Fangs slashed his shoulder. Buster's own teeth had pierced his lower lip as his face hit the ground. His nose felt numb. Getting up and defending himself seemed oddly unimportant.

His head cleared. He knew that he'd been out cold, if only for a second. He felt no weight on his back. He heard growling. He rolled over with his knife ready in his hand.

"Well. Thanks, Ace," he mumbled, wincing at the pain in his lower lip.

Trooper lay flat on his back, his throat fully exposed. Part of one ear had been torn off, and blood matted his coat. The Labrador straddled him on stilted legs, growling whenever the shepherd dared to twitch a muscle.

Buster motioned Ace away. Trooper got up slowly, favoring his right front paw. Buster examined it. The bone showed, but the leg wasn't broken. His other injuries, as well as Buster could determine through the thick coat, weren't serious. The torn ear ruined his show dog handsomeness, but Buster didn't care about that; he felt this was an improvement.

"Well, you stupid asshole, I guess you know who's top dog around here, right?" Tentatively, Trooper wagged his tail. "Yeah, it's okay, you got carried away, that's all. Otherwise, you did fine today. Now sit there till I tell you."

He dressed the doe quickly. He divided the warm liver in three, chewing on one piece while he worked. He hadn't eaten since yesterday morning, and a pang of real hunger struck him at the first taste. He tossed the next biggest piece to Ace, then the last to Trooper. They waited alertly for more, but he ignored them as he did a rough butcher job with his knife. He made a bag of the doe's hide for the cuts he wanted and slung it over his shoulder.

Still chewing on the raw liver, he walked into the woods, the dogs at his heels.

Chapter Two

Buster wheeled slowly through the graveled semicircle in front of Pete's Tavern. He had gone home to clean up and stow part of the meat in his freezer, but it was still only a little after noon. Aside from Pete Jensen's, there was only one car in the lot, a mud-splattered station wagon. He saw that it had New York plates. He chuckled softly.

"Maybe we can scare us a tourist," he said to Trooper. "If you bite him, you get to keep him."

He drove to the back of the building and parked near the door of the kitchen. He let the dogs out of the back seat and watched them romp toward the woods in a snarling sham battle. There were no hard feelings between them.

A sudden and black despair gripped him. They were only dogs. The rapport he had felt with them and the deer, just before the kill, had been a fantasy. He felt no bond with them now, no connection with any other creature. He was completely alone.

He backed off and dealt his car a savage kick. That feeling of being a part of all life – not an isolated consciousness but a receiver of all impressions – he had felt it before, usually during a good hunt. And before, as now, he could never recapture nor recreate the feeling by simply remembering it. It was only an illusion.

The dogs had stopped their play to watch him. He snapped his fingers to call them. over. He told Ace to wait by the car and guard it. That wouldn't be hard for Ace, because he could smell the meat in the trunk. He took Trooper with him as he walked around to the front of the building.

"What I need is a piece of ass," he said.

Funny he should think of that. Good sex, and the letdown that came after it, were similar to the experience he was now trying to understand. Sometimes it felt as if his consciousness were dissolving, blending with that of the woman he was screwing, but the feeling never seemed real when it was over. Peggy Jensen was a pretty good lay. He hoped she would be at home while her old man was minding the roadhouse.

He let the screen door slam behind him as he walked into the big, low-ceilinged room. When his eyes had adjusted to the dimness, he saw bald-headed Pete talking with a customer at the bar. He had hoped the tourist would have a woman with him, some city woman he could show off for, maybe scare a little bit, but he seemed to be alone. He was big, but pale and flabby, with bushy black hair and horn-rimmed glasses.

Buster sat at a table near the bar. He was disappointed to see Peggy swinging toward him, a tall girl with wide hips and blunt fingers and a lot of dyed blond hair.

She shot a guilty glance toward Pete, then put on a real smile. "What can I do for you, Buster?"

Loud enough to be overheard, he asked, "Do you serve Jews in here?"

"Cut it out, Buster. Please."

"No, I'm serious, I want to know. Do you serve Jews

in this place?"

"Of course we do. Now, behave yourself."

"Well, then, I'll have a beer, and my dog here will have a Jew."

Peggy turned red and dissolved into giggles. What a stupid cunt, he thought, but he faked a loud laugh as he repeated the punch line of the old joke. The customer didn't rise to the bait. He kept on eating his hamburger and staring at the bottles behind the bar.

Pete called out, "I told you, Buster, keep the Hound of the Baskervilles out of here. It's against the law."

"The law is a ass," Buster said.

The stranger perked up at that. He turned on his barstool with a tentative smile and said, "Dickens."

Blank-faced, Buster stared at him for a moment, then turned his back. His heart wasn't in the game. The customer was ten years older than he was and looked like a real pussy. He didn't even have a woman with him. What was the point?

"That all you want, Buster? A beer?"

He switched his attention back to Peggy, who stood close. She toyed with her order pad as if she were the belle of a Victorian ball toying with her fan.

"Ayuh, you can tell your old man I got a load of meat for him, out in the car." He let a sly smile spread on his face. "I got some for you, too. You want it now, out in the car?"

"Buster!" she hissed, glancing fearfully at Pete; but he knew Pete hadn't heard, and so did she.

She went to the bar, putting extra emphasis into the swing of her hips. Buster watched one cheek clench, the other relax beneath the flimsy pink cloth of her tight uniform.

"What's his name?"

Buster looked at the customer uncomprehendingly. He resembled a mole, with his round shoulders and long nose and thick glasses. He wore a red polo shirt that called attention to the roll of flab at his gut.

"Huh?" Buster grunted.

"The dog. What's his name?"

"Storm Trooper."

Trooper sat up straighten at the sound of his name. His good ear, and the scabbed shred of the other one, flicked erect.

"That's a good name," the customer said, "for a dog."

Buster studied him. He was smiling. Maybe he just didn't know the rules. Maybe he was used to swapping clever insults with other pussies in some fairy cocktail lounge. Right now, the last thing he expected was a fist in the face. He was close to getting it.

Getting no response from Buster, he switched his attention to the dog. "Here, Trooper. Come here, boy. You want a peanut?"

Buster tried hard not to laugh, but he couldn't help himself. Pete laughed too.

"You better not call him, Dave," Pete said. "He might just come."

Buster turned back to Peggy when she arrived with the beer. Without thinking, he removed the baseball cap he had been wearing low on his forehead before he reached for the beer.

"My God," Peggy said. "Where's you get those shiners?"

"Had a fight with my dog."

"I believe it. You and them fucking dogs."

"You bite his ear off, Buster?" Pete asked. "Is that how you won?"

"Yeah. Tasted better'n anything I ever ate in here." In an undertone, he added, "Present company excluded."

"You better cut that out," she whispered with stiff lips.

He checked Pete with a flick of his eyes. He was jawing with the customer again. Before she could react, he ran a hand up Peggy's dress and lightly caressed her crotch with two fingers. She squeaked and jumped back, but Buster's surprise was as great as hers. His fingers had encountered only soft hair and softer flesh. The unexpected contact aroused him suddenly and totally.

"You bothering the help, Buster?" Pete called, but he said it with a grin of pure cowardice.

Buster ignored him and drank his beer. It stung his split lip. Peggy's wide brown eyes reminded him of the doe's, just before he had slit her throat.

"Get yourself a headache or something," he mumbled. "I want you now."

"Sure," she said. "Okay."

"You want that stuff, Pete, or don't you?" Buster asked. He drained his glass and banged it down on the table.

"Yeah, sure. Give me your keys, Buster, I'll take care of it."

"No, you won't, old buddy. Ace is guarding the car." He got up and put on his baseball cap, hiding his face with the creased bill. Trooper sprang to his feet at Buster's first move. "Come on with me, we'll get it."

He didn't glance at Peggy as he left by way of the kitchen.

Chapter Three

Dave Stern sat alone at the bar, nursing his beer and wondering if he should have another. He pushed the button on his digital watch, an impractical Christmas present from Carol. The red numbers were invisible in sunlight, but the watch was fine for telling time in dark bars. Maybe she'd been trying to give him a message. It was only a quarter to one. He would hang around a little longer.

He looked at the solidly built waitress, Pete's child bride. Normally placid and dull, she looked distraught. He wondered if the weird little man with the washed-out eyes had upset her.

"You okay?"

"Yeah. No. I got a headache. You want something?""

"Another beer, I guess. I can wait for Pete. What's he doing with that guy?"

"Search me," she said unconvincingly.

Dave didn't care; he was only trying to make conversation. As he had thought, it was difficult. He wondered what an educated man like Pete saw in her. He smiled as the answer to the silly question came immediately to mind.

"I'll get your beer," she said. Her strong hand trembled at the tap. She spilled more than she poured, and what she poured was mostly foam.

"You make me homesick for Coney Island," Dave said, pushing a wet bill toward her.

"Huh?"

"Nothing."

Pete came back, hitching up his belt over his overflowing gut.

"Honey, I all of a sudden got this splitting headache," Peggy said. "Is it okay if I go home?"

"Sure, baby. Shall I eat dinner here, or – ?"

"No, I'll be better by then. You come home."

"See you, baby," he said, patting her sturdy rump.

Pete rested his heavy forearms on the bar as he watched her leave, his face full of pride and admiration.

"Put some beer on this head, won't you, Pete?"

"Aw, shit, sure. Sorry." Pete drew the beer carefully and said, "Listen, I should've told you. Don't get wise with Buster Callan. He's nuts."

"What would he do, give me a punch in the knee?" Dave laughed. "He's kind of small for his age."

"You should've seen what he did to two guys, both bigger'n you, out in the parking lot one night. He's a fucking maniac. I'm telling you. And that dog of his would swallow you whole and spit out the buttons." He hesitated. "I'm sorry about that joke he made, that Jewish thing."

"I didn't like it either, but you don't have to apologize to me. I'm not Jewish."

"Oh." Flustered, Pete concentrated on wiping down the bar.

Dave was annoyed with himself. At thirty-six, why did he still have to volunteer that information? It shouldn't have mattered to him whether anyone thought he was a Jew or a Hindu or an Eskimo.

"Who is he?"

Pete brightened. "What is he, that's the question. If you were to call him a son-of-a-bitch, I suspect you would be making a simple statement of fact. He talks to his dogs."

Dave shrugged. "I talk to my dog. Doesn't everybody?"

"Yes, but do you expect answers? And do you get them?"

"Buster does, huh?"

Pete brooded for a moment. "Sometimes I almost believe it, the way he's got them trained. His other dog, Ace, can count. Buster'll have me put a certain number of glasses on the bar and say, 'How many glasses do you see, Ace?' And old Ace'll go 'Woof!' for each glass. After six or seven, he sometimes gets confused, but he can count up to five at least as well as Buster can. They both win a lot of free beers that way. Maybe there's some kind of a trick to it, but you have to admit it takes a lot of natural talent and hard work to train a dog like that. If Buster wanted to make a business of it, breeding dogs and training them, he could probably make a good living, but steady work isn't his line."

"What does he do?"

"He was left a small farm, but he doesn't work it. He guides when he can, or poaches, or steals things. Once in a while he'll do an odd job, like painting houses or doing carpentry work."

Dave was silent, momentarily unable to think of a substitute for the question he wanted to ask: why had Pete taken fifty dollars from the register and gone out back with Buster? The answer didn't matter to him. He didn't care whether Pete had lost a bet, or whether he was receiving stolen goods, but his ignorance underlined the fact that he was an outsider. He had lived here for almost a year, and Pete was the only person outside his family with whom he could hold an extended conversation, but even those conversations were constricted by the limits of barroom sociability. And Pete wasn't even a native.

Dave said, "Seeing somebody like that, I wonder if I'll ever be able to fit in up here. I mean, it would be as easy for me to strike up an acquaintance with a man from Mars –"

"Hold on, I think you accidentally hit on the truth. Mars is most likely where Buster came from. He's not at all typical of the people around here. He wouldn't be typical of any place, except maybe a bughouse."

"Yeah, but you're able to talk to him."

"It's my job, I run a bar," Pete said. He noted Dave's wry smile and hastened to add, "I know how you feel. Folks around here are very standoffish. They consider you a newcomer if your grandmother and grandfather weren't both born here. I ran into the same thing myself, but I overcame it. I even married a local girl."

"Well," Dave said, draining his glass, "you have an advantage. You make great hamburgers."

"That's true," Pete said. "You can't get a hamburger like that in New York City."

Chapter Four

Dave Stern's father had been raised on a farm in Minnesota. He had run away from its grinding poverty and back-breaking labor as soon as he'd been able to, but he'd later filled Dave's head with romantic notions about the virtues and pleasures of rural life.

Until Dave was twelve, the Sterns lived in a rural backwater of New Jersey and raised chickens. Their place couldn't really be called a farm, but its memory and his father's stories had given Dave a feeling of nostalgia for the soil that he'd never been able to shake. He always considered himself a country boy at heart.

After they moved to a house in town, Dave's father gave him a .22 rifle for his fourteenth birthday. Sometimes his father would drive him to an abandoned gravel pit where they would shoot at tin cans, and he would tell Dave stories about his boyhood hunting and fishing adventures in the Great North Woods. Such trips were rare, though, because Dave's father preferred to spend his spare time in bars and horse parlors.

As a child, Dave was a voracious reader. His favorite books were those of Jack London and Edgar Rice

Burroughs, authors who wrote enthusiastically about the wilderness. They shared the view that man had lost touch with the better part of his nature when he had opted to live in towns, or even in houses.

When Dave was sixteen, his father dropped dead of a heart attack while trying to encourage a laggard at Aqueduct. Dave was deeply grieved. He knew that his father had been an unhappy man, and he believed that his unhappiness had been mostly due to the combination of economic pressures and bad luck that had forced him to spend most of his life in the industrial heart of the Eastern seaboard.

The year after his father died, Dave undertook a strenuous program of roadwork and calisthenics, then set out alone to hike the Appalachian Trail. He had never been very athletic. He had never spent a night outdoors. He found that he loved it.

He thought about studying forestry or veterinary medicine when he went to college, but science and math were not his strong points, so he majored in English. Bored and short of money, he dropped out in his second year. He got a job with a newspaper and got married. Still longing vaguely for the country, he found himself being drawn ever closer to the city. For a year or so he would go hiking on weekends or on vacations, but Carol, his wife, didn't care much for the sport, and he gradually lost interest in it himself.

When the hippies emerged on the scene, Dave itched to join a commune in the wilderness and grow organic foods. Carol wasn't entirely unsympathetic to the idea. They talked it over long and earnestly, but in the end they decided against it. He was doing well at his job. They had two young children to think of. For a year or so, Dave sported a beard and, on his days off, wore sandals. Carol stopped using home permanents and began cultivating marijuana in a window box. On Sunday, Dave would always read the ads for farms and country properties in the *Times,* but he never answered any of them.

Dave could write glibly on any subject. He had an unpublished novel in the bottom drawer of his dresser. One day a newspaperwoman told him that she'd been supplementing her income for years by selling stories to women's confession magazines. If she could do it, so could he, but was nevertheless astounded when his first effort, which had cost him only a few hours' work, brought him a check for a hundred dollars.

He began a serious study of the magazine field. Soon he was selling fiction and articles to a wide variety of publications, although his knack for writing confession stories – a talent that embarrassed him – remained his most saleable asset. When the newspaper where he worked abruptly went out of business, he decided not to look for another job, but to become a full-time freelance writer.

Carol was skeptical. Only one percent of all the writers in America, she never tired of reiterating, actually made a living from writing alone. Dave disarmed her criticism by taking a conscientious and businesslike attitude toward his work. He became the toughest boss he'd ever had, putting in ten hours a day at writing, interviewing, or researching. His spare time reading included nothing not related directly to his work. He wrote a lot, and he was able to sell most of it.

After two years of this, his income was half again what his newspaper salary had been, and even Carol was willing to acknowledge his success.

At first, Dave refused to admit what his success meant: namely, that he could live anywhere he pleased. He struggled against that notion. He told himself that he had to live in New York and maintain personal contact with the editors who bought his stuff. The objection couldn't stand up to close scrutiny. It was true that he made some sales because he was near the center of the action, but most of his business could just as easily have been conducted by mail or telephone. He was forced to acknowledge that he was free, and that freedom scared him.

Most of all, he was scared of putting his comfortable old dream to the test of reality. He paced around the prospect of a new life in the country, tested it, sniffed at it like a zoo animal unwilling to believe that the keeper has left his cage open.

At last he broached the subject to Carol, and he was amazed to find that she had been thinking along the same lines. She had always loved the city with a passion that Dave had never shared. Those friends who had moved to the suburbs she had regarded as deserters from a noble cause.

But lately even her New York City chauvinism had cooled. Their neighborhood, once middle class, could now charitably be described as sleazy. Pushers dealt openly on a nearby corner. They knew six people, and had heard of others, who had been mugged in the lobby or the self-service elevator of their apartment house on West End Avenue. Walking a few blocks on Broadway now meant running a gauntlet of winos, panhandlers, perverts, and lunatics. They had a bitter laugh when the *Times* reported that urban blight had officially spread below Ninety-Sixth Street on the Upper West Side, because they lived several blocks above that frontier. The rats had deserted the ship, Carol said – referring to friends who had long ago fled to the suburbs – and now perhaps it was time for the human beings to think about leaving.

The kids were old enough now to be included in their parents' deliberations. Alice embraced the idea enthusiastically. At fourteen, she was passionately dedicated to God and horses, and she felt she stood a better chance of encountering one or the other in the country. Mark, who was two years older, surprised them. Nothing ever ruffled his cool, and he never spoke to adults in anything but grunts, but this time he delivered an ultimatum: he wouldn't go unless he got a car. Dave and Carol agreed. The money they would save on private school – tuition wasted on Mark anyway, since he was a poor student and wanted to become a heavy-equipment operator – could buy a couple of cars.

That settled, there remained a wide area for negotiation. Carol's idea of the country extended only to some bucolic suburb of Stamford, where the city would still be accessible for one-day shopping or theater excursions. Dave was thinking in terms of Alaska, with the Ozarks as a second choice.

Dave had seen Vermont as a compromise. Now that they were there, it was becoming increasingly clear to him that Carol hadn't. Her present attitude seemed unfair. She had been awed by the weary old humps of the mountains, delighted with the postcard prettiness of the neat little villages, none of it much changed from Dave's boyhood hiking memories. When they had found the eighteenth-century farmhouse, hidden away in the midst of an orchard on the lower slope of a modest mountain, she had declared herself in love with it. The price tag of eighty thousand dollars only partly cooled her ardor.

That was a sore spot – money. Carol had inherited a portfolio of stocks from her parents, and its sale had provided almost the entire down payment on the house. She had always spoken of it as *their* money, hers and Dave's, but he never forgot its source. Her brother, during a heated exchange with Dave, had reminded him more than once where the money had come from. Dave's brother-in-law, Paul Warren, had told him he was a fool to sell the stocks in a depressed market. Dave had argued that land would always be a safer investment than stocks. Paul was a successful businessman who had always patronized Dave as an impractical eccentric, and had done it so well that Dave always felt uncertain and defensive with him. His own doubts had made him shout all the louder at Paul. It had been a nasty scene, brought to an indecisive close by Carol's hysterical tears.

Refighting that argument and chewing over the clever things he should have said, Dave abruptly found himself at home. His driving had been automatic. His grip on the steering wheel had been so tight that his hands ached when he relaxed it.

He cut off the engine and made a determined effort to calm himself. The orchard was in bloom again, just as it had been when they'd first set eyes on the place. It was odd how people could accustom themselves to beauty. He never would have thought it possible to pass through the foamy white bounty of the gnarled apple trees without responding to the sight, but he'd just done it. Even now, consciously trying to appreciate the display, he was irked by the knowledge that the promise of the apple blossoms was a false one. The trees were old, the land exhausted, and the apples would be few and small and sour.

The pervasive clucking of the chickens filled his ears as soon as he got out of the car. He'd forgotten how noisy and smelly they could be. But they had all the fresh eggs they wanted, just when doctors were warning that more than one or two eggs a week could be harmful. Dave tried to scoff at such warnings. His hens had laid the eggs, and, by God, he would eat them. He ate two every morning.

He went to the back of the wagon and opened the tailgate. He could still chuckle at the sticker Alice had plastered there, but it was partly a chuckle of embarrassment: PROTECT THE RIGHT TO ARM BEARS. Such a sentiment, he believed, wasn't popular in this part of the country. Maybe Buster Whatsisname had seen it and objected to it, and that's why he'd come on to him with such hostility at the bar.

He couldn't remove it, though, not without wounding Alice. She'd barely spoken to him for a week after he'd impulsively bought the .300 Savage. At the time it had seemed a necessity for his effort to get back to nature, to a more simple and direct life, to the wilderness that his father had known. He had looked forward to going out and stalking a deer, killing it, and proudly bringing the meat home to the tribe. The tribe hadn't appreciated his first step in that direction. Alice's wide-eyed gaze had accused him of planning to murder Bambi with an elephant-gun. The sour set of Carol's lips told him he'd squandered money they couldn't afford to waste. Mark had examined the gun for a few minutes, showing a slight lessening of his chronic boredom, but he hadn't even suggested they go out and take a few practice shots. The rifle stood by the kitchen door, unfired.

Buying chicken feed had been the primary purpose of Dave's trip. He shouldered one of the sacks just as Rags came out to give him a belated greeting. Rags was an Airedale. According to tradition, the breed had been developed by poachers. Dave wondered what Buster, allegedly a real poacher, would have thought of a dog like this. He laughed at the idea as he clapped Rags on his fleshy flanks. Never mind guns, fireworks made him shake like a leaf and scramble under the bed. Back in the city he'd hated to walk in wet weather. He would try to lift all four feet off the pavement at once. Alice had bought him a set of strap-on boots that seemed to please him. He balked at the coat she'd also bought him, though, after he'd received his first shock of static electricity.

He stowed one bag on the back porch and returned to the car for the other one. Hands free, he could engage in a tussle with Rags, who snarled and slashed without ever letting his teeth make contact. Dave had thought the dog would soon shed his fussy, epicene ways in a more natural environment, but the country seemed to make him even more neurotic. Let out to romp, he would sulk under the porch and seize the first opportunity to run back into the safety of the house.

Maybe Buster would know what to do about Rags, how to drag him out and make him relish his new freedom. He was supposed to be a genius with dogs. Maybe Buster's hostility would fade when he recognized in Dave a fellow dog-lover. It might be a chance to make a friend in this unfriendly place. Pete had called him crazy, but Dave didn't give much weight to that diagnosis. Eccentric, certainly, and suspicious of strangers – that would be a more likely description.

In their brief encounter, Dave had recognized him as a man of action, a type he had always admired, envied, and never fully understood. Only once or twice in his own life had he plunged headlong into action on impulse, without pausing to weigh the odds, and those times he had felt good. Buster probably lived every minute of his life like that. If he could win his confidence, he might tell him about that life, tell him about the technical aspects of poaching. He might prove to be a gold mine of material that Dave could use for stories or articles.

He dumped the second bag on the porch and walked into the kitchen, nearly stumbling as Rags shot between his legs to gain the security of the house. He was out of breath from the minor exertion of carrying the bags. He felt bloated and sleepy from the three or four beers he'd drunk with his hamburger. He would have to do something about getting himself back in shape – but that was an empty threat, he knew from experience. Now he felt more like taking a nap than anything else, but he could hear Carol running the vacuum cleaner upstairs.

He went to his study, a side porch that he had enclosed last summer. Doing that sort of work had left him little time for his writing. Then winter had come, and with it all sorts of unforeseen emergencies, including a power failure that had lasted two weeks. It had thrown him off his stride, and he'd never managed to get back into his old work habits.

He winced as he read the sheet in his typewriter. He had been working on one of his true confession stories. He couldn't bear to read his own gluey prose, nor to think about the insipid narrator he had created. But he had to. He sat down at his desk.

"Oh. There you are."

Carol stood at the door, looking hot and tired. A red bandanna concealed her tawny hair, and that drew attention to the elegant bones of her face. He congratulated himself, as he often did, on making such a good choice of a wife. She looked better at thirty-five than she had at eighteen.

But his pleasure at seeing her gave way to the memory of an earlier annoyance. "You weren't cleaning Mark's room, were you?"

"If I didn't do it, it would never get done."

"Damn it, there's no reason why he can't make his own bed and vacuum his own room. He's seventeen years old, and you have enough to do."

"Not really," she said, coming over to the desk and taking one of his cigarettes. "It's a habit, a routine. I can clean the whole house without thinking about it. Where'd you put the groceries?"

"Oh, shit."

"That means you forgot, huh? You took enough time. Where were you, shooting the breeze with your cronies at the Dew Drop Inn?"

"We've gone through all that. How can I write about

people if I never get to talk with any?"

"With a bunch of inbred, degenerate shitkickers?"

"Come on, now," he said, somewhat more sharply than he'd intended. He was angry with himself for using such a flimsy excuse, angry with her for making him produce any excuse at all for his idleness.

"Give me the keys," she sighed. "I'll go to the market."

"They're in the car."

He worked, but part of his mind was free to think about Carol. They loved each other, but their brief exchange had been devoted exclusively to complaints. He resolved to try harder when he saw her again.

Three pages later, he heard Rags barking happily. The car door slammed: He wrote two more lines to finish the page he was working on. Three pages of two-hundred-and-fifty words each, at five cents a word: thirty-seven dollars and fifty cents. He had probably made less money during Carol's absence than she had spent.

He came out to the kitchen, where she was propping two bags on the table. "Is there more?" She nodded, and he said, "I'll get it. How much did you spend?"

"Fifty-one something."

"Damn. I'll have to write another page today."

"At least."

He was halfway to the car before he felt the sting of that remark.

When he returned with the remaining bag, Carol was putting groceries away with decisive briskness. Cans banged, bottles clinked. Her mouth was set in a tight line.

"I was kidding," he ventured. "What's wrong?"

"Nothing. Nothing at all. It takes a load off my mind, it really does, knowing you feel so secure that you can afford to sleep until eleven o'clock in the morning and then spend two hours in a bar. We must be doing really well."

He went to the stove and lit the burner under the coffee pot. She was making it hard for him to keep his brand-new resolution. He supposed that he'd started it, though, by asking her how much she'd spent. She must have read an implied criticism into the innocent question. He came up behind her and laid his hands on her shoulders. She was stiff and tense, but she made no move to shrug his hands away.

"Don't be sarcastic. Something's wrong, and it's got nothing to do with when I got up or how long I spent in a bar. Tell me straight out, maybe I can fix it."

"I don't know what's wrong, that's the trouble," she said. "Oh, yes, I do. I'm sick and tired of going to that damned supermarket and finding nothing but Maxwell House on the coffee shelf. I'm sick of Tuna Helper. I want an exotic spice. I want a cup of Earl Gray tea. I want to read the Sunday *Times* on Saturday night, not on Wednesday afternoon. And while all those rotten cows are stinking up the countryside, I can't even get sour cream."

"You know that they've always ordered things for you when you asked."

"Sure, but asking them makes me feel like a foreigner or something. And I am. I ask for things that nobody else would think of wanting. And the things I ask for – they're just junk I've been conditioned to like. I feel like a machine that's been programmed to drink Chock Full O' Nuts, and a buzzer goes off if I don't get it."

He slid his arms around her waist and rocked her gently as the tension left her body. He tried to conceal his unexpected arousal by her. It seemed inappropriate.

"Culture shock, that's what it is," she went on. "I go into that damned supermarket in my ratty old jeans with a bandanna on my head, and here are all these women dolled up like Tammy Wynette, because it's the only place they ever go. One of them kept staring at me as if she thought I was a dope-crazed killer."

"Maybe it wasn't your outfit. Maybe she was one of those inbred degenerates you were talking about."

"Hey, ow," she cried when he grabbed a handful of her buttocks. "Cut that out."

"Why?"

"Because I'm hot and tired and depressed."

"It's a sure cure for depression," he said, but he let her slip away. He went to mope over the coffee pot, which was not yet sufficiently heated.

"I'm sorry I took it all out on you before," she said. She resumed putting groceries away, but without her earlier vehemence. "I just wonder what's *me*, and what's important and what isn't."

"Maybe we ought to go and spend a week or so in the city, when school lets out."

"Maybe," she said, but without any real enthusiasm.

He stared through the windows over the stove at the blue panorama of mountains. A movement in the foreground caught his eye. At the side of the house, a stream had been damned to form a pond fifty yards across. A doe and two dappled fawns had come out of the woods beyond the water.

"Look," he said. "Look there."

Carol came to his side at once, drawn by the urgency in his voice. She watched as the doe lowered her head to drink and the fawns frisked beside her.

"That sort of makes it worth all the trouble," he said. "Doesn't it?"

She didn't answer, but she took his hand and squeezed it as she watched.

Chapter Five

Buster waited in the car, just out of sight of the roadhouse, tapping his fingers on the wheel in time to the country music on the radio. He was glad that he'd washed up before going to Pete's Tavern. It hadn't occurred to him until he'd gotten there that he might get a piece of Peggy Jensen. It looked like a pretty good day all around.

"Oughtta get you guys a bitch, too," he told the dogs, who listened attentively. "Only you'd just fight over her."

He believed that women were a pain in the ass, but Peggy was different. She was tough and independent. She didn't try to change him in any way. She didn't get the sulks when he neglected her for days or even weeks on end. She didn't yap at him when he wanted quiet.

She wanted nothing from him but a good fuck every now and then, and she gave as good as she got.

Peggy's drunken father had knocked her up when she was thirteen. He was never punished for it, and he kept on alternately screwing her and beating her until he drank himself to death a couple of years later. Freed from his jealous supervision, she soon made a name for herself as the town slut.

When Pete Jensen came to town with money falling out of his pockets, looking for a business to buy, she cleaned up her act and aimed herself at him like a rifle. He didn't stand a chance. Everybody got a laugh out of that: Peggy Rambo, the hottest piece in two counties, rigged out like a blushing bride for a sucker old enough to be her father. They were placing bets to see when she would make her first misstep.

She surprised them all. Everyone had predicted that she would lie around the house all day, figuring out ways to spend Pete's money while she entertained her old boyfriends, but she pitched right in and went to work for him at the roadhouse he'd bought. At first she had to ride out a lot of winks and pinches and coarse jokes from the customers, but she rode them out with the cool dignity of a queen forced to wait on the peasants. Before very long, men got uneasy about winking at her or reminding her of the good old days. They felt embarrassed, as if they'd confused her with somebody else.

And she played out the whole script without letting Pete know what was going on, as far as anybody could see.

Like nearly every other boy in his high school class, Buster Callan had given Peggy Rambo his virginity. Unlike the others, he had never been cut off. Maybe that was because he never asked anything from her, either. Maybe it was because she knew he would never boast to his friends about it, since he didn't have any friends. And maybe she liked him, the same way he liked her. He'd never bothered to analyze their relationship. He never thought much about her when she wasn't around.

He got a glimpse of her in the rear-view mirror and turned to watch her striding down the road on long, strong legs. She'd got herself knocked up a second time, when she was in high school, but nobody knew who was to blame for that. Maybe he was. He used to wonder about it.

Her first pregnancy had been aborted, but she decided that she wanted the second one. She wanted to stay in school, too. The principal wanted her out. A welfare lawyer argued her case before the school board, and he convinced them that he would make more trouble than it was worth if they tried to expel her.

She waddled out of class one Friday afternoon, looking as if she ought to have running lights to warn traffic, and she was back at her desk on Monday morning. slim and as full of the devil as ever. She'd had the baby and released it to an adoption agency over the weekend. If she'd been a man, Buster would have said she had balls for brains. That was the highest praise he ever gave her.

"Took your time," he said as she opened the door and slid onto the seat beside him.

"I had to wash up." She slipped her arms around him and kissed him. She broke off the kiss when he was just getting warmed up and said, "I forgot about your lip. Does it hurt to kiss?"

"Yeah," he said, pulling her back and plastering his mouth to hers, kissing her so hard that she tried to squirm away.

"I hope you washed the good part." He faced front and switched on the ignition.

"That's what I meant." She giggled. "It ain't easy in a sink."

As he drove, he put his hand beneath her dress and stroked her bare thigh. He never grew tired of touching her skin. Among the few women he'd known, her skin was unique. It was as soft and as fine-textured as silk, and yet he could feel firm muscles beneath it. The nearest thing he could compare it to was stroking Ace's puppy-soft fur and feeling the steel of his muscles underneath. He knew she wouldn't like that comparison, no matter how well intended it was, so he said nothing. Nor did the comparison hold up, not all the way, because he would turn himself in if he ever got a hard-on from petting Ace.

She moved her legs apart, inviting him to move higher. He glanced at her. She lounged on the seat as if asleep, her head back, her eyes closed. He saw wrinkles around her eyes that he'd never noticed before. She was his age, almost thirty. It made him sad to think of her growing old. He tried to remember exactly how she'd looked in high school, and he couldn't.

He slid his hand all the way up. She purred. She was already damp. He rubbed her the way she liked. He could make her come two or three times like that, and she would still want the real thing. She said that Pete didn't give her enough. He drank too much, he was always tired when the time came, and half the time he couldn't get it up. His inability would embarrass him, and he would either pretend to be asleep or else pick a quarrel with her and stalk off to sleep on the couch.

She claimed that she was unable to please herself this way, that it just didn't work. Buster found that hard to believe, she came so easily when he did it. She was coming now, saying "oh oh oh," her face red and sweaty. She pushed up from the seat, swabbing herself against his fingers, then sank back, gasping. He stroked her thigh.

"That was nice," she said. He said nothing. He unzipped his fly. She began to caress him with her fingertips.

"Where we going?" she asked.

"Down," he said, and he pulled her by the nape of the neck.

He concentrated on the road while she worked. This was one thing she could do well, far better than any of the whores he'd paid to do it when he was in the Army. She used her lips and her teeth and her tongue all at once, all in different ways.

He glanced back at the dogs. They were hanging out the back windows, their ears flapping in the wind. Funny how they didn't seem to care what people did. They weren't at all curious about human sex.

"Damn damn God damn!" he yelled, hitting the steering wheel. "Oh!"

She sucked a little longer, then sat up and arranged her dress primly. She sat with her hands in her lap, smiling slightly. Her lower lip was very thick, and maybe that's what made her so good. She was good at kissing, too.

"Like I said, where we going?"

"I figured we'd go to my place."

"That's good. I don't like to do it in the woods, with the damn dogs watching."

"They don't care. I was just thinking about that, that they don't give a shit what we do. People are different. They'll even pay to watch."

Peggy laughed. "They don't pay to watch dogs."

"That's a good point. But I saw this movie once where a woman got fucked by a dog."

"Don't talk dirty like that. It's disgusting."

"Okay, it's disgusting. I'm just telling you what I saw. Then a pig fucked her and he was better at it. You could tell he was really enjoying himself. It was this place with movie machines in New York City. You could just walk in off the street and put your quarter in a machine, and you saw stuff like that. The movie would go black at a good part, and you'd have to feed another quarter to the machine if you wanted to see any more."

"I suppose you'd like to watch your dog do it to me, and that's why you're telling me all this. Forget it."

He laughed and slipped his arm around her shoulders. She squeezed closer quickly.

"Shit, no. I'm just telling you what it's like when they let the Jews run things, like in New York City."

She blew air past her lower lip in exasperation. "That kind of dumb talk is even worse. Honest to God, Buster, sometimes you make me sick. Like with that man in the bar."

"A goddamn kike. So what?"

"It doesn't matter what he is. He's an American, just like you or me. And he's not a bad guy, he comes in there all the time. He always treats me like a lady."

"Maybe he is a lady."

She pulled back and gave him a punch in the ribs. It hurt, but he didn't show it. Ace roared at her, and she recoiled.

"You better watch that stuff. He'll take your fucking arm off."

She threw a contemptuous glance at the dog and then ignored him. "That just goes to show that what I said before is true. He must know what we're doing when we make love. If he thought we were wrestling or something, he'd bite me. So that's why I don't like to do it in the woods with him watching."

"You're doing a lot of bitching today. You want me to take you home so your husband can wave his limp dick at you?"

"No," she said, flinging her arm around him and snuggling against him, pressing her ample breasts against his sore ribs. "Is your house all messed up?"

"No more'n usual."

They turned in at his place, where a faded sign advertised his services as a guide. The rusted hulks of several automobiles that had been cannibalized to keep the one he was driving running littered the front yard. The one-story house had been slapped together by various hands over several generations. Part of it was faced with logs, part with tarpaper, and part with cedar shakes. The roof was mostly corrugated iron. He kissed

Peggy before he climbed out of the car and freed his dogs.

"C'mere, Trooper. You get tied."

Peggy got out and stretched. "How come?"

"Dumb bastard'll go chase after deer and get himself shot. Or cows. I know what's in his mind. Ace knows better than to get into trouble."

Trooper allowed his collar to be fixed to a heavy chain. Ace bounced up the steps and waited by the door with his tail wagging.

"Sorry, pal." He fended off Ace with his knee while Peggy slipped inside. "Show's over for today."

The house smelled musty and sour, even to his nose. It had been a long winter; and he hadn't gotten around to giving the place the airing it needed. Peggy didn't complain, though. She opened the glass doors of the bookcases and sat on her haunches to inspect the titles.

"You got a lot of books," she said, "I never noticed."

"They been around a long time."

"Pete's always got his nose in a book. Even when he watches TV. He even takes them into the bathroom."

"So do I."

"Not those kinds of books." She giggled. "I seen the books in your bathroom."

He sat in a lopsided chair and began to unlace his boots. She had reminded him that he would have to send away for some new magazines. The ones stacked in the bathroom had lost their zest. To hell with it, that was just money down the drain that he couldn't afford. The real thing was far better, even if he got it as seldom as he did.

"War books. Adolf Hitler. The Holy Bible," she recited as she moved her finger down a shelf. "Dickens. Is that what he meant?"

"Who?"

"That guy in the bar. You said something, so he turned around and said, 'Dickens.' He meant you were quoting from Dickens, right? He was just trying to be friendly, to make small talk with you."

"He's an asshole, and was just showing off. That's all. Since when have you been interested in books? Why don't you do something useful, like take your clothes off?"

She ignored him. Even she had her contrary moods, and he hoped she wasn't working herself into one. He took off his shirt, balled it up, and threw it at her. She pretended not to notice as she pulled out books at random and leafed through them. Her chunky rump stretched her pink skirt as she squatted, and muscles stood out on her pale legs. He felt a hollow need in his gut as he studied her.

"More war. More Hitler." She dusted off her hands and shook her head in disapproval, then closed the bookcase. "I read mostly magazines. *Modern Romances,* and stuff like that. Some of them are like real life, only everything always works out all right in the end."

He grunted as he pushed off his jeans.

"I sent them one I wrote once, it was a true one about . . . oh, never mind. They sent me back a note saying the idea had been used too much before. Only it wasn't an idea, it was true, except for how it ended, with everybody seeing how what they were doing was wrong and promising to change their ways." She turned and saw that he was naked. "Buster, you're terrible!"

"Terrible? I figure it's a compliment, if I get this way just from looking at you with all your clothes on. Come on over here."

She came over and perched on his knee. While they kissed, he undid the fastenings of her dress and her bra and pulled them down. Her elaborate hairstyle was a trap for cooking grease and tobacco smoke, but he didn't mind. He associated the odors with her; they reminded him of other days when they had made love.

"Is your bed made?"

"What do you think?"

She blew some stray hairs out of her eyes and got up, fending off his caresses. "I'll go do it."

He sat and watched her for a moment. Her behind jiggled more than it used to, but it still never failed to excite him. He got up and followed her into the bedroom, where she was tidying the rumpled bedclothes. He came up behind her and entered her while she was leaning over the bed.

"You bastard!" she cried, and she tried to break away, but he pushed her down and held her.

"What's the matter? You're ready."

"I don't like it this way, you know that."

"I like to look at your pretty ass when I'm doing it."

"And I like to look at your ugly face. You just want to do it like the dogs. I think you are part dog."

"That's a compliment," he said.

She didn't say anything more. She pulled her knees up onto the bed and relaxed beneath him, eyes closed, gasping to the rhythm of his strokes.

He lay back and stared at the stains on the ceiling, the map of an imaginary world where he often waged wars, while Peggy smoked a Marlboro.

"You got to air this place out, Buster. It ain't still winter, you know."

"I will when you finish smoking that thing."

"You'll never do it." She got up, the cigarette dangling from her lip, and started to remove the plastic sheets that covered the windows. "You want to save these?"

"I guess. They don't give them away."

She could never be a model for one of those magazines. Her hips were too broad and her breasts were beginning to sag. She was probably way over the hill for such purposes; anyway, since most of the girls looked as if they were in their late teens. It didn't matter. They were probably all whores, and wouldn't be nearly as congenial as Peggy. Nevertheless, he sometimes wondered what it would be like to have a girl like that.

Peggy opened the windows and carried the plastic sheets out to the kitchen. He rolled off the bed and leaned out of one of the windows, breathing deeply and looking around for Ace. He didn't see him. When he turned back into the room, she was changing the bedding.

"Regular fucking housewife."

"Somebody has to do it," she said. "You got to take all this stuff down to the laundromat, too. That's one thing I can't do for you. When did you change these sheets last?"

"You did it, the last time you were here."

"Come on, Buster, that was Halloween!"

He laughed. "Was it? Well, that's when they got changed last."

"I guess I ought to feel good about that. It means you sure as hell ain't had no other girls up here. Nobody else would stand for it. I remember it was Halloween, because I went to this dumb party with Pete and left him there to come and see you."

She picked up her bra from the chair where she'd left it and started to untangle it, but he came up and slipped his arms around her waist.

"Come on, Buster, I got to be there when Pete comes home for supper."

"We got time for one more," he said, and he turned her in his arms and pushed her back toward the newly made bed as he kissed her hungrily.

"One more," she whispered. "Yes."

Chapter Six

Now that she'd vacuumed the house from top to bottom, had even clamped on the seldom-used attachments to clean odd corners and crevices, Carol had no legitimate way to block out the clacking of the typewriter. It was against the rules to play the stereo or the television loudly when he was working.

She could have listened to records with earphones, but she refused to do that. Staying in one place and wrapping herself in a cocoon of sound would have been a surrender to boredom and irritation. She was half-afraid that she would never be able to extricate herself from such a cocoon.

She had to keep moving, not just for the sake of the activity itself, but to make the old house sparkle. Getting up this morning, seeing dull disorder all around her, she had known that she was looking at a map of her own mind. By brightening the map, she just might alter the dreary terrain that it represented.

She had already waxed the dining room table, the gate leg table in the living room, the Shaker cabinet in the bedroom, the frame over the fireplace that held a reproduction of Wyeth's *First Snow.* She had beaten the hooked rugs until their colors were once more vivid against the dark glow of the wide-planked living room floor. Now she was scouring the fireplace hardware. And listening to that damned typewriter.

As a steady background noise it would have been bearable, but its ragged rhythm was in continual collision with the frayed edges of her nerves. Long silences would lull her, and then she would jump when the staccato rattle began again. He seldom typed steadily for more than three or four minutes at a stretch. Then he would stop. Rat-tat-tat. Pause. Rat-tat-tat-tat.

The sound had never bothered her in the city, but there it had been buried in the universal din: the racket of the elevator near their front door; the telephone that kept ringing in an empty apartment down the hall; the blood feuds that were aired in six languages in the street below; and the fire engines erupting through 106th Street with a pandemonic chorus that could have been justified only by another Dresden. Here, the typewriter had no competition. Its rattle intensified the enormous silence around it.

She scrubbed harder at the big brass kettle that held the fireplace tools and tried to pin down the time when the noise had first bothered her. Not at first, no. Even though her brother had done his best to ruin their new life for them on the eve of their departure, and even ruin their marriage, he had succeeded only in dampening her spirits for a while. She had soon cheered up, diverted by the fresh newness of her surroundings, kept busy with the million little details of making a new home.

The power failure, four of five months after they moved in, had been the high point of their lives here. It had been like a two-week picnic. Three days after it started and the county road had been plowed, a volunteer fireman had come to ask them if they wanted to be evacuated. Dave had nonchalantly declined, managing to give the impression that the fireman was offering to guide Dan'l Boone out of the woods. She had felt a warm pride in her husband glow in her then, even though she was doubtful about staying.

Indoors they wore blankets over their sweaters and coats, and they resembled some order of squat and bulky monks dedicated to a rule of extreme personal discomfort. Dave and Mark went out every day to cut wood with a two-man saw, returning red and laughing and exhausted in the crystal twilights with loads of logs to feed the gluttonous fireplace overnight. She and Alice were kept busy collecting buckets of snow to melt for cooking and washing.

In the evenings they would huddle around the hearth, singing or playing Scrabble or reading aloud by the orange glow of kerosene lamps. Dave, a real ham at heart, was inspired by the atmosphere to choose his readings from Poe and H.P. Lovecraft, adding suitably maniacal chuckles at the most gruesome passages. One of the Lovecraft stories, about hideous creatures lurking in the remote hills of Vermont, had scared the wits out of everyone, including Dave.

They would retreat into their goose-down sleeping bags early, before ten o'clock, and she never slept more soundly in a comfortable bed than she slept those nights on the floor. Sometimes, floating just beneath the surface of consciousness, she would sense that Dave had gotten up to feed the dying fire.

She remembered one night when she awoke fully to see him tending the hearth. Their eyes met. It was strange how they felt mutual and spontaneous need, and each knew just how the other felt. He came to her in her sleeping bag. Maybe the proximity of the sleeping kids, making it seem dangerous and wicked, maybe the primitive conditions . . . whatever it was, it was great.

Two or three times Dave put on his old backpack

and made the six-mile hike to the general store for items whose need they hadn't foreseen in planning for a winter emergency.

She worried about him. Quite bluntly, he was in lousy shape, and younger men than he had dropped dead from unaccustomed exertion. He laughed at her worries, but eventually he hired someone to plow their driveway and the mile of unimproved road to their house.

It was perverse, certainly, but it felt good to worry about him, to indulge herself in the unfashionable fantasy of Pioneer Wife. You hardly ever got a chance to worry about a man who hung around the house most of the time, clattering away on a goddamned typewriter. It was soon after that, when things returned to dull routine, that she'd started resenting the sound.

She set down the brass kettle that she'd been buffing automatically, realizing that Captain Bligh himself would have considered its shine excessive, and examined that word: "resented." Had she meant that? Did she resent the fact that his typing was the sound of real work, that he was actually doing something to bring in money, while she was polishing brass and waxing floors and growing old and bitchy?

No, that was too simple. Such a thought sounded like the revelation of some young twerp at her first consciousness-raising session. She didn't resent his making money. She'd contributed her share, too, and it was about time he made some. What she resented – what she envied, really – was his ability to ignore the bland green threat of the lovely, emptiness surrounding them, to shut her and the kids and the whole world out of his head – and become, for a few hours each day, Sally Fudd, the teen-age nympho, baring her tortured soul for a readership of gum-chewing housewives in pink curlers; or Rob Masterman, risking death in the alleys of Marrakech to win the explicitly described embraces of a voluptuous houri, to tickle their onanistic husbands. Dave's surroundings simply didn't matter to him, because he had an escape route as effective as schizophrenia or LSD in that typewriter. And she, rooted hopelessly in the here and now, had none whatever.

She rose, refusing to admit the twinges in her knees were anything new, and took Rags's tennis ball – no, damn it, it wasn't his tennis ball, it was hers, but where could you play tennis in this desolation or find anyone with whom to play it? – and bounced it once. The dog appeared instantly, skidding one of the hooked rugs into a crumpled pile, and danced around her on his hind legs as he tried to seize the ball.

"Outside, you pervert," she said, keeping it from him with difficulty as she went to the front door. "That's where you're supposed to play ball."

Rags loved the words "play ball" and hated the word "outside," and his struggle with this antithesis subdued him, but he followed Carol out the door. On the porch, she leaned back and flung the ball far out into the orchard. He streaked after it.

She pulled a cigarette from her chambray work shirt and lit it before confronting a fact she had been avoiding. Her resentment of Dave's typing had begun shortly after the power failure had ended, but that hadn't been the cause. The immediate cause, she recognized now, had been Jack's phone call.

Rags, without the ball, returned to the edge of the orchard and barked furiously at her.

"You're absolutely hopeless!" she yelled, and she knew she was partly yelling at herself and the universe, as well as at Rags. "Won't you feel ashamed when I find it? A human being?"

She walked down to the orchard and Rags scoured the ground ahead of her; hoping to find the ball before she could. It was odd how her mind worked. It seemed as if the tennis ball had reminded her of Jack, but she knew her thought processes had been more devious than that. She had been suppressing his memory, and she had tricked herself into picking up the ball.

Cissy Parker had talked her into taking a quarter-share in a tennis court rental two summers ago. The court was laid out in an unused warehouse in the Village; the floor was uneven, one of the baselines was flush with a wall, and consequently it was cheap. It even seemed worth the often-harrowing ride on the Seventh Avenue IRT.

The third share belonged to Brad Stein, whom Cissy always cloyingly referred to as her "roomie," and the fourth was held by a cadaverous model named Riga Thorssen. Riga's assignments were unpredictable, so she almost never showed up, sending her friends, her friends' friends, or her friends' friends' acquaintances. Carol tried to get Dave to take Riga's place, but he wasn't interested.

Jack Prewitt had never even met Riga, but her network drew him in and he started coming regularly, eventually buying out the model's share. He was a good player, a pleasant companion, but not the sort of man Carol would have given a second glance in other circumstances. He was ten years younger than she, and his concerns and attitudes and interests seemed immature. He taught at a private school in the Village, but he didn't seem especially bright.

Despite all that, she was flattered by his obvious interest in her. It amused her to encourage him while keeping him at arm's length, like a frolicsome and affectionate puppy. When they stopped off for drinks after their Monday afternoon sets, she would find herself behaving like half a couple with Jack, a social balance to Brad and Cissy.

She hadn't planned anything. One day it just happened. Brad and Cissy had to run off, but she went to the White Horse with Jack for the customary drink. One step inside the door she hesitated, annoyed to find the place crowded, annoyed by an overly loud ballgame on the television set. Either Jack shared her feelings or else he read her reaction instantly. When he suggested they have their drink at his place on Perry Street, she accepted without a second thought.

Her second thoughts came later, during the short walk to his apartment, but she didn't have the nerve to hurt his feelings by refusing his invitation on what would seem a whim. If she changed her mind, it would spoil their light, bantering friendship, it would have made them forever self-conscious with each other. Besides, Jack was just a harmless kid. She could handle him.

Unexpectedly, it was herself that she couldn't handle. His first kiss was no surprise, but her own response was. It seemed as if she'd been expecting it and yearning for it, without suspecting her own desire, ever since she'd met him. It would have been difficult to retreat from the emotional level of that first kiss, nor did she try. He proved to be gentle and considerate and very, very good.

She took the Broadway local all the way home to give herself time to think. It was her first infidelity in sixteen years of a more or less equable marriage. Why had she done it? Another gray hair detected in the mirror that morning, a quarrel with Mark, petulance from Alice, inattention from Dave – no, those were no reasons at all. She'd done it partly because she didn't, deep down, think of Jack as a real person: he was an amusing toy, a harmless dodo, and it was so easy to be totally relaxed with him, totally herself, totally in control. . . . Basically, she did it because she wanted to, and she would be damned if she'd feel guilty about it.

Rags snapped her back to the present with an imperious bark that said he wasn't going to hunt for the ball if she was going to drape herself over an apple-bough and stare off into space.

"Okay, okay, we both miss the city. Do I yell at you for hiding under the porch?"

She wandered forward, kicking the grass aside near the place where she supposed the ball would be. She refused to think about the ticks and snakes and God knew what, tarantulas, that might be lusting for a bare human foot to bite. Rags saw the ball before she did. After a symbolic show of independence, refusing to let her have it, he dropped it at her feet. She threw it further down the slope of the orchard.

Jack had called her at . the apartment the next day, but she had ended the call almost brusquely. She had, in her stay-at-home husband, a built-in excuse for not talking to Jack. He had called again – lunch, a drink, anything, a walk in the park, any chance at all just to talk to her – but she had kept on refusing.

However, she did show up for, tennis the following Monday. So did Jack. She could have made her escape from him by leaving the White Horse when Cissy and Brad left, but she didn't. She went to his apartment again.

She had thought of the first time as a misstep, perhaps, but as a misstep she was entitled to. Everybody, she had told herself, deserved at least one little moment of glorious irresponsibility. After the second time, she could no longer look at it that way. She was a married woman who was having an affair with a much younger man. It was at once deliciously wicked and shabby and sad, and she loved every minute of it.

Dave never suspected a thing, thank God. It would have torn him up. Despite his intelligence and his liberal instincts, he had never entirely risen above his strait-laced, blue-collar background. That was why he could write those stupid confession stories so well. Deep down inside, a part of him really was Sally Fudd.

He never bothered to ask why she now went to Balducci's in the Village for specialty foods she normally would have bought much closer to home at Zabar's. He didn't think it odd that she developed an interest in old movies at the Elgin or the Bleecker Street Cinema, always the films that he had seen too many times or had never liked. She needed to make fewer flimsy excuses after that September, when she transferred Alice to the school where Jack taught. Dave didn't even question the decision.

As a Virgo, she had always been rather, strait-laced herself – *prissy*, that was the word that Dave had flung at her during one of their rare arguments. Dave had been her first lover, on their wedding night, and she had always imposed certain limits on their lovemaking. With Jack it was different. Since he didn't matter to her, not really, she could be free with him – a paradox, certainly, but that's the way it was. The only restraints she imposed on Jack were to forbid him to talk about love or spin out fantasies of the future. In a way, those were the cruelest conditions she could have set down, because she knew that he was falling ever more deeply in love with her.

She tried to ease her conscience by deferring to Dave in almost everything. She became more attentive around the house, more responsive in bed. Often she would find him gazing at her with a look of profound affection, and it was like a knife twisting inside her.

It had to end. She was sick of plotting and scheming and covering her tracks. She was sick of living with the constant fear that Dave would find out. Worst of all, she was developing – well, not love for Jack, but an emotional dependence on him, a need for him. It was pointless, it was futile. Half of her wittiest remarks sailed a mile over Jack's head, and he never said a single witty thing. He would never understand her the way Dave did. They could never share the same emotional depths.

It was Dave who gave her the answer to the problem. In one stroke, he gave her a way to ditch Jack and, at the same time, to absolve herself from guilt by making a sacrifice for him that he didn't even know he had coming. The solution? – pack up and move to Vermont.

Even now it was painful to remember the last scenes she'd played with Jack. She resolved to be firm with him, even brutal, and she had been. And then, the very next day, she'd called him up to apologize. Seeing her waver, he pushed hard for what he wanted her, as his wife, his mistress, anything, on any terms. More cruel scenes followed, more apologies, tears, letters back and forth, phone calls. She would never know how Dave failed to notice the knockabout farce, or tragedy, or whatever it was, being passionately played out behind his back.

At last Jack had given up, or seemed to. No love, she told herself, could have survived the lacerations of that final month. She had dedicated herself to making a new life, a new home, and in the closeness and love she'd felt when they were snowbound, she'd congratulated herself on her success.

Then Jack had called – "I love you"; "No, you don't, you dodo!" – and since then she hated the very sound of her husband's typewriter.

Rags had no trouble finding the ball this time. He dropped it at her feet as soon as he returned, eager to keep the game going. She knelt to hug his thick neck and bury her face in his woolly coat, but he would have none of that. He squirmed away and barked at her:

She was about to tell him what she thought of him when she heard the sound of Mark's car coming up the drive. The sound of the Datsun was distinctive because, he said, there was a sewing machine under the hood. She pulled the bandanna from her hair and dabbed it against her eyes, then strode briskly up to the yard to meet her children.

Rags trotted along with the ball in his mouth. Why had she packed those tennis balls, when she'd known that she was going to be a hundred miles from the nearest court? For Rags, of course. Of course.

Mark was disengaging his bulk from the car. He was big and dark, like his father, but there was none of Dave's gentleness in his square jawed face and sullen eyes. Dave looked Jewish, though he wasn't, and Mark looked like a hit-man for the Mafia, even though there was no Italian in his ancestry; and, despite his sinister looks and surly manners, he was even more of a pussy-cat than his father was.

Alice, running to meet her now, was the wild card: fair and blue-eyed, with two dark-eyed parents. She had a fair grandparent on either side, though, and that accounted for it, unless you wanted to flirt with madness and think of her as blue-eyed Jack's retroactive child.

God. When Alice was born, Jack was ten years old.

Having given her a kiss on the cheek, Alice pulled back and asked, "What's the matter, Mom?"

"Pollen," Carol said, and she blew her nose noisily into the bandanna. Perceptive little witch.

"Mark wants a van, but I figure it's my turn first, and I get a horse, right?"

"Where are you going to keep a horse?" Mark asked. "You need a stable."

"There's all these farms around, and farmers. They'd rent out the space, wouldn't they, Mom? Maybe they'd even let me have the space for free, if they weren't using it."

"Anyway, your horse would cost money, and my van would just mean trading in this sewing machine and making up the difference, which I've got, so the one's got nothing to do with the other," Mark said, with the air of one lecturing an idiot.

"You don't have that much money," Alice said. "You'd have to get some from Dad."

Mark shrugged, and Carol looked at him sharply. His allowance seemed to multiply like the proverbial loaves and fishes, and she was almost certain that he was dealing grass to his classmates. Up here, that would probably get him the electric chair. It was one of those things she'd been meaning to talk to Dave about.

Mark hurried into the house. Perhaps he'd realized that he'd said too much and sensed what was on her mind.

Alice slipped her arm around her waist as they went up the steps together. Carol had never supposed, when she named her daughter for Lewis Carroll's most beloved heroine, that her Alice would grow up to look like Tenniel's pictures of that Alice – well, not quite perhaps, at least not anymore: her Alice would never have gotten down the rabbit hole with a bust like that. Just this year, she had burst flamboyantly out of childhood.

Carol had anticipated problems from uprooting the children and taking them to the country, but they had never developed. Alice had loved the idea from the first, and even the reality hadn't disappointed her. It alarmed Carol to note how her daughter's speech was developing a Yankee twang. Mark had made the necessary adjustment with his usual, unflappable cool. But Dave was at loose ends, to say the least, and she – well, she was going up the wall.

If only Dave hadn't come up with that well meant but damnably ill-timed idea of going to the city for a week!

"Hey, what happened to Rags?" Alice asked when they were inside.

"He must have come in with us, or with Mark. He wouldn't have stayed out."

"Yeah, but must've. I'll go look. – Hey, Rags!" Alice cried, flinging her books at the bentwood rocker and missing it as she ran to the rear of the house.

Carol sagged against the doorframe for a moment. The living room was once more resembling a map of her mind. She shoved herself forward to straighten out the rug that Rags had disarranged. She picked up Alice's books and stacked them on the gate leg table. She didn't feel like doing anything about Mark's tracks on the freshly polished floor.

She was distracted by Rags's barking, coming from outside. It had an unfamiliar quality, an almost hysterical note. She hoped to God Alice hadn't ordered a horse, that it wasn't arriving now, COD.

She had planned no, not planned, she was incapable of planning anything anymore – she had wanted to spring that idea on Dave herself, of going to New York for a week. Alone. Jack was still waiting. He had called twice more since that first time, despite her protests. He knew enough to call in the morning, when Dave was sure to be asleep, when she could talk, when she could say things like – God, she'd actually said it, she hadn't dreamed she could – "I love you, too, you dodo."

Outside, Alice screamed. She kept on screaming.

Carol ran, nearly colliding with Mark and Dave as they squeezed out of Dave's study together.

"I don't know what it is," she said, answering thc silent question they both asked as she pushed past them and raced through the kitchen.

"Mom! Oh, God, Mom, look, it's awful, it's horrible! Daddy!" Alice screamed when Carol reached her at the side of the house. "Daddy!"

At first Carol just saw a wild confusion of tumbling, bloody animals on the far side of the pond. She had to stare for a moment before she could sort it out. A pack of wolves – no, dogs, all different sizes and colors

– were pulling down a stag at the water's edge. The stag kept wheeling and turning, head down, menacing the dogs with his broken antlers. The dogs worked as a team, some rushing him from the front while others tried to sneak up behind him. The stag's movements were slow and clumsy, as if his exhaustion were almost complete. His flanks and hindquarters ran with blood. Rags, on this side of the pond, kept barking furiously, and Alice never stopped screaming.

"Jesus," Dave breathed as he came up beside her. Then he sprinted back into the house.

"Where's he going? What's he doing? Daddy!"

"Getting his gun, I bet," Mark said with an almost total absence of boredom in his voice.

"Don't look, honey, don't look," Carol said, pulling Alice to her and holding the girl's face against her breast.

But Carol watched. The stag's head shot up. A spotty dog, perhaps a Dalmatian, flew into the air. He landed on his back with a thud that was audible even at this distance. Carol was surprised to see him get to his feet.

While tossing the Dalmatian, the stag had turned his back for an instant on a black monster that had been hanging on the edge of the struggle. The black dog shot past the stag like a cannon ball, leaving a gaping red wound in one of its hind legs. When the stag started to turn, the leg crumpled beneath him. Instantly the dogs covered him like a writhing, snarling blanket. Only his head remained visible. Mouth open. Screaming.

"Holy shit," Mark said, his voice choking. "They're eating him *alive!*"

Alice looked, despite Carol's efforts to restrain her, and she began screaming again. The stag regained his footing and shook most of the dogs off. His whole hide seemed either black with blood or red with wounds. The black dog hung from the stag's neck like a nightmare leech, his grip unbreakable.

"What are you going to do, Daddy?" Alice called as Dave ran past them with his gun. "Daddy?"

"Shoot him. Put the poor bastard out of his misery."

"No, Daddy, no! Shoot the dogs! Maybe we can do something for him, maybe he can be well again."

Carol started to speak, but Mark spoke first, "His back leg's broken. See, you can see the bone sticking out. He's already dead."

"He's right, honey," Carol said.

"No! Those dirty, fucking dogs –" Her words dissolved into sobs, and Carol decided it was no time to criticize her language.

The dogs hung back, but their ring was much closer than it had been before. Some of them sat, tongues lolling, waiting. The light-colored dogs showed bright blood on their muzzles. The black horror still clung to the stag's neck, and the deer's efforts to shake him were listless and ineffective.

Dave was halfway across the weir. The weir. Carol had fallen in love with that word a long time ago. It had come as a delightful surprise to her to realize that they actually owned one, that the earthen dam at the foot of the pond was an honest-to-God weir. She would have enjoyed springing the word on her friends – but she never saw her friends anymore.

Rags, still barking, was following Dave at an extremely safe distance. The pack watched them. Some of them took off immediately. Others hesitated. One, a collie-type mongrel, took a few stiff steps toward Dave with his fangs bared. Dave raised the rifle and fired. The sound was shockingly loud, and it sent echoes rolling across the pond.

"God *damn!*" Dave shouted in frustration.

Vandals had once flung a Halloween pumpkin at Carol's speeding car from a highway overpass. The pumpkin had hit the front of the hood and exploded, disintegrating into a cloud of flying fragments. She was reminded of that moment as she saw what the .300 savage did to the black dog's head. End over end, the headless corpse was thrown a dozen yards from the deer.

All the dogs were fleeing now as Dave fired again. The stag collapsed in a jerking heap. Rags ran forward to claim the field.

Chapter Seven

Dave crossed the weir with the rifle cradled in his arms. Common sense told him that the pack was already in the next county, but the back of his neck was impervious to common sense. He felt the chill of erected hairs.

The stag was unquestionably dead. Some of its ribs and the bones of one hind leg showed bare and white. The dogs had done so much damage that he couldn't, without kneeling down for a closer look, find the entry wound of his bullet. He didn't want to kneel down for a closer look. A fly crawled on the deer's staring eye.

"You okay?" Mark asked at his shoulder.

"Yeah. I'm. . . ."

His mouth went suddenly sour. In the next instant he was vomiting, leaning on his rifle and whooping for breath while Mark patted his back.

"Nerves," Mark said coolly. "A nervous reaction."

Christ, he felt like a fool. Mark was right, but it was humiliating to be comforted like this by his teen-age son. He wiped the tears from his eyes and stole a glance across the pond. Carol and Alice had gone indoors. He hoped they hadn't seen. He straightened up. His guts squirmed, but he had them under control now.

"What'll we do with it?" Mark asked.

"Bury it."

Mark shrugged. "We could eat it."

He wondered if his son was trying to make him sick again, but it was impossible to detect any malice in his drowsy expression.

"I don't think your sister would like that idea."

"I'll skin it, if you want."

Mark turned and went to examine the dead dog before Dave could answer. How could his son have spotted his weakness so clearly? The thought of cutting into the deer's flesh, even touching it, repelled him. So much for the mighty hunter and his daydreams of a "natural" life.

He couldn't understand his own reaction. It was illogical; it was even out of character. As a newspaperman, he'd seen dozens of dead bodies – human bodies – in all stages of mutilation and decomposition. He hadn't been immune to those horrors. He used to have nightmares about some of the things he'd seen. But he'd never reacted like this before.

Of course, he'd never seen anything being killed before either, being torn apart before his eyes. Nor had he ever shot a living creature. Those thoughts cheered him a little.

He tried to turn his squeamishness into a joke. With more confidence in his voice, he said, "The idea of finishing up the dogs' dinner doesn't grab me."

Mark ignored his words. He said, "This dog belonged to somebody. I thought they must've been wild."

Dave walked to the carcass of the dog. Rags, extremely subdued, was sniffing it suspiciously. Mark handed Dave a collar with a license attached. The leather was well worn, but it was obviously of good quality. It was also stained with blood.

"Maybe he ran away and went wild," Dave suggested.

"No, somebody's been taking good care of him. He's in good shape." Mark suddenly giggled. "For a dog without a head, that is."

"I didn't mean to shoot him," Dave admitted. "I was aiming for the deer. The gun shoots to the left, I guess."

"The son-of-a-bitch got what was coming to him," Mark said, standing up and giving the black dog a perfunctory kick. "He could've stayed home eating his Alpo."

And I, Dave thought, could have stayed in New York eating my Häagen-Dazs. He felt utterly out of place in this scene of butchery, holding this heavy rifle. Mark's unruffled acceptance of everything appalled him.

"Go get a couple of shovels," Dave said. "We ought to bury them before they stiffen up."

Rags was worrying a piece of the deer, and he put up a struggle when Mark tried to drag him away by the collar. He finally consented to go when he'd torn off the piece he wanted. He held his head high as he trotted after Mark with his gory trophy.

It took more than an hour of hacking through roots and dislodging rocks to dig even a shallow grave. The stag's antlers wouldn't fit in the hole they'd dug, and at first it seemed they might have to saw them off, but Dave succeeded in wrenching the animal's neck back until its antlers lay parallel with its spine.

Looking down at the stag, he was struck with a weird feeling of déjà-vu. It took him a moment to recall that he'd seen a stag posed in the same way, with its head flung back, in a reproduction of a prehistoric cave painting. He smiled ruefully. He was a far different creature from the man who had painted that stag.

He got the body of the dog and dumped it on top of the deer.

"Aren't you going to throw in his collar?" Mark asked as they began filling in the grave.

Dave thought for a moment. "I ought to find the owner, and tell him what happened. Maybe he won't let his next dog run loose."

"He'll probably sue you. Everybody around here thinks we're rich."

Mark might have been right, but Dave decided to keep the collar. He felt guilty about killing the dog. Owning up to the act would relieve some of his guilt. Perhaps the dog had belonged to a child who was even now calling it for supper.

They returned to the house in the twilight of dusk with blood on their clothes and blisters on their hands. In the kitchen, Dave immediately poured himself a large scotch over ice.

"I'm sorry I screamed at you, Dad," Alice said, stretching to kiss his cheek. "I couldn't think, it was all so horrible."

He patted her shoulder abstractedly as he took a gulp of his drink.

"I called the police," Carol said.

"Huh? What for?"

She answered with unexpected vehemence. "Because that could just as easily have been Alice that pack of dogs was chasing, or somebody else's kid. And kids can't run as fast or as far as deer can."

"Aw, come on. They wouldn't have hurt anybody. They were just house-pets with big ideas."

"Like the one that growled at you? He would have attacked, if you hadn't fired the gun."

"I was interrupting his dinner, that's all. Rags'll growl at you if you try to take a bone away from him. It's no big deal." He paused to take another sip. She didn't look at all convinced by his reasoning. "What'd the cops say?"

She smiled without humor. "They shared your view, that I'm a hysterical female –"

"Carol, I said nothing of the kind!"

"– an alarmist who doesn't understand dogs." She glared at him for a moment. In a milder tone, she added, "If you found tags on the one you killed, they said you should take them to a game warden."

He didn't know what to say to her, not yet. She had found another reason to hate the country. He wished she hadn't found it so soon after yesterday's outburst. Her imagination had probably now filled the surrounding hills with roving packs of ravenous hounds.

He dug the collar out of his pocket and dropped it on the table. "He did have tags, as a matter of fact."

Alice, perched on a corner stool, had been listening quietly. Now she said, "Would they do that to a horse?"

"I don't think so, honey." He finished his drink and poured another. "Horses and dogs get along, from what I've heard." Unexpectedly, he remembered just what it was he'd heard on the subject, a long time ago. His father had once told him that certain racehorses became attached to dogs, that some horses were unmanageable unless a favorite dog was sharing the same stall. Seeing that Alice was still watching him, he added, "Anyway, a horse is bigger and faster than a deer."

He went to the kitchen closet and got his gun-cleaning kit, then sat down and jacked the remaining shells out of the rifle. The operation made a lot of noise in the silent kitchen, and he was acutely aware of Carol's eyes on him.

"What are you doing?" she asked.

"Cleaning it."

She looked at him oddly.

He felt the need to elaborate. "You're supposed to clean a gun after you fire it."

He wished he knew what was eating her. Something was, something that went a lot deeper than this evening's incident. He began to feel that he was being treated unfairly. He had behaved well today. He had done what had to be done to the wounded stag. He had chased off the pack that she considered so dangerous. He had been able to do those things only because he had bought the rifle she hated so much. Christ, John Wayne couldn't have done better!

Maybe John Wayne wouldn't have botched it by accidentally shooting the dog, and he certainly wouldn't have thrown up when the shooting was over, but those were unimportant details. He deserved some praise, a kiss, anything but this display of unfathomable bitchiness.

Alice – this kind of treatment from her would have been understandable. After all, he'd just blown Bambi away, right before her eyes. Maybe she didn't approve of what he'd done, not entirely, but she'd come around to a sensible acceptance of it. She'd even apologized for her emotional reaction, which surprised him, because he hadn't even noticed it at the time. She caught his eyes on her and gave him a flicker of a smile.

"There's a name here," Carol said. She was studying the inside surface of the collar, holding it close to the lamp on the kitchen table. "W.H. Callan. And something else, an address probably, that I can't read."

"I'll look him up tomorrow," he said. The name was vaguely familiar. He must have seen it on some rural mailbox.

"I wouldn't," Carol said. "Leave it to the game warden, that's apparently one of his jobs. By the way, the police said you did the right thing. It's okay to shoot a dog if you see him chasing a deer."

Perhaps that was supposed to be a compliment, but her tone was flat and uninterested.

"I didn't want to shoot him. He was only following his natural instincts."

Carol didn't comment. She let the collar rattle to the table and lit a cigarette. He concentrated on running the cleaning-rod in and out of the barrel. He hadn't smelled the distinctive odor of *Hoppe's #9* since he was a boy, and it brought back clear memories of his father and the .22 he'd given him.

If Carol hadn't been so determined to be a thorough pain in the ass, this would have been one of the most contented moments of his life.

"Daddy," Alice said timidly into the uncomfortable silence. "We talked about it before, remember, and you said to talk to you some other time, and . . . I mean, I was wondering, can I have a horse?"

"Sure, honey," he said, keeping his eyes on Carol. "What color?"

He had the satisfaction of seeing Carol wince, but then his view was blocked as Alice flung herself on him and all but choked him with the violence of her embrace.

Chapter Eight

Dave supposed that he could have found the local game warden or the owner of the dog he'd killed in the phone book the next day, but he preferred to ask Pete Jensen. It would give him a chance to talk about what he'd done. Nobody at home wanted to listen.

Carol's mood had passed, though. He'd had a few more drinks after dinner; he hadn't been drunk, but if he'd been perfectly sober he wouldn't have made any advances to her last night, She'd surprised him by accepting him readily, even eagerly.

Later, as they held each other in a light embrace, she apologized. The dogs had scared her, she said, but the rifle scared her even more. She had an irrational – her word – horror of guns. She'd had it as long as she could remember, but it had been reinforced by the assassination of President Kennedy. Seeing what the rifle could do, then watching him *fondling* it in the kitchen – she'd wanted to scream.

"Fondling" annoyed him, but he knew better than to quibble with the word. He kissed her, apologizing for his thoughtlessness. He couldn't help wondering why she hadn't told him all this before, why she hadn't expressed her feelings with more force and precision when he'd bought the damned thing, but he didn't ask.

Finally she told him what he'd been wanting to hear: that he'd done a fine job, that she was proud of the way he'd acted. Even though he'd been waiting for it, the compliment embarrassed him. He felt obliged to confess how he'd been sickened by the results of his shots. She was delighted with his confession. She hugged him tightly.

It had been a sweet, tender exchange, and he was still buoyed by it that morning. She hadn't even raised the subject of Alice's horse, and what it would cost them. She would, though.

It was shortly after noon when he got to Pete's Tavern. The dining area was moderately crowded, but the barstools were empty. He sat near the service area, where Pete was mixing drinks and ringing up the cash register.

"Hello, Dave. Beer?"

"Yeah." He surveyed the room from his barstool. Two waitresses he didn't know were working the floor. "New help?"

"Aw, Peggy's under the weather again. You want a hamburger? I'll –"

"No, no, I just stopped by on my way here and there." He sipped his beer. "You don't know anything about horses, do you, Pete?"

"'I know two things about a horse,'" he quoted, "'and one of them is rather coarse.' If you want to place a bet, I could direct you, but that's about all."

"No, my daughter wants a horse, and I don't know the first thing about buying one, or keeping one."

"They sell them at auctions, I think."

"You're a big help." He waited for Pete to finish a transaction with a waitress and settle down, arms folded on the bar, before he said, "Had some excitement yesterday afternoon. A pack of dogs chased a deer into our yard."

"Yeah?" Pete looked interested. "They'll do that, all right."

"They were tearing the poor bastard up. I had to shoot him. Shot one of the dogs, too." He saw no point in mentioning his poor marksmanship.

"How many dogs were there?"

"Six or eight, all shapes and sizes."

"You should've shot a couple more at least. They'll just go and do it again."

Pete took his glass for a refill and was distracted by an order for Bloody Marys. His absence gave Dave a chance to get over the mild annoyance he'd felt at Pete's reaction.

"I only wanted to scare them off," he said when Pete returned with a beer. "Maybe I taught them a lesson."

"Not likely," Pete said. "People try all sorts of things to keep their dogs from running deer. Like tying a piece of deer meat around the dog's neck and letting it rot, so that he can't stand the smell. Or putting the dog inside an oil drum with some deer meat and beating on the drum with sticks, or rolling it down a hill. There's this woman, Mrs. Wallace, out on Beaver Dam Road, who has a Dalmatian that runs deer. She got a remote-controlled electric collar, and if the dog took off after a deer while they were walking in the woods, she'd zap it. But all that dog ever learned was not to run deer when its owner was around. Shooting the fuckers, that's the only cure."

He was unprepared for the obvious depth of Pete's feelings on the subject. An enthusiastic hunter – his reason for moving to this part of the country – perhaps he regarded dogs as unfair competition.

Pete added, "The State of Maine patrols for dogs with helicopters, and they shoot any dog they see running a deer. Or probably any dog they see, period. That's the way to do it. Look, I've got a hunting dog myself, a Weimaraner. I keep him in a fenced-in run, and when I take him for a walk, he goes on a leash. If he got loose and started chasing deer, which he probably would, and some guy shot him, I'd shake his hand and thank him."

Not sharing Pete's enthusiasm for shooting dogs, Dave made a noncontroversial comment. "There was a Dalmatian in this pack."

"See, what'd I tell you? Mrs. Wallace has the only Dalmatian within fifty miles of here. And that dog's been given shock therapy. A couple thousand more volts, that's what it needs."

"The dogs are only following their instincts," Dave said, "just like the hunters."

The remark nettled Pete. "Now, don't start on hunters. You won't see a hunter chasing a pregnant doe until she miscarries. Or coming around in the wintertime and driving a herd away from their forage so they starve to death. And when was the last time you saw a hunter hacking off pieces of a deer while it was still alive?"

"That's what the dogs were doing yesterday," Dave admitted. "But I'm sure the stag didn't feel it. He must've been in shock."

"You don't believe that any more than I do," Pete said scornfully. "Suppose they gave you your choice of a way to die, being shot or being torn to pieces by a dog. You'd pick the dog, of course, because you'd be in shock and you wouldn't feel it."

Dave laughed. "Whether I believe it or not, there's a certain emotional –"

"Oh, bullshit," Pete interrupted. "I'll have to admit, there are some hunters who shouldn't even be let outdoors, but you won't find many of them who'll kill an animal and walk off to let it rot. They've got some use for it, even if it's only for the antlers to hang over a fireplace. But dogs'll often chase a deer till it drops dead of exhaustion, then trot home for their dog food without touching the deer."

He could have pointed out the shallowness and inconsistency of Pete's arguments, but it probably would have meant staying there all day. He finished his glass, and Pete refilled it before he could decide whether he wanted another or not.

"Anyway, what am I trying to convince you for?" Pete said when he returned. "You shot the dog, I didn't. That one's on me. By the way, what did you do with the deer?"

"Buried it. What else?"

Pete opened his mouth as if to say something, then apparently thought better of it.

"I buried the dog, too," Dave said with a touch of sarcasm; but a waitress put in another order at that moment, and the remark went unnoticed. When Pete returned, Dave said, "Do you know anybody named W.H. Callan?"

Pete laughed. "Yeah, the W.H. stands for Wild Hair. That's Buster. You saw him in here the other day."

Dave's dismay must have shown on his face, because Pete stopped chuckling. "His other dog," Dave said slowly, "the one that drinks beer and counts. What kind of a dog is he?"

Pete stood back from the bar. He looked suddenly pale. "A Lab," he said. "A black Lab."

"Oh, shit," Dave sighed.

"Oh, shit, is right. Christ Almighty? Have you told anybody else? Anybody at all?"

"No, but I figure I better tell him."

Pete grabbed his arm and leaned forward. Urgently, his voice lowered, he said, "Don't do that, whatever you do. I mean it. Just forget about it, forget it ever happened."

"I can't do that. He's probably worried about his dog. Maybe I could even offer to pay for it, I don't know."

"You'd pay for it, all right," Pete said, shaking his head.

"To tell you the truth, Pete, it was an accident. I was aiming for the deer. I think I ought to do something about it."

"Accident. What you're going to do, you're going to get yourself accidentally buried somewhere back in the deep woods. I'm not kidding you. I'm not exaggerating." Pete paused to pour himself a large shot of cognac. "Buster's nuts, genuinely nuts, and he's dangerous. That dog meant a lot to him. He lives alone in that run-down house of his, he doesn't drink much, he doesn't gamble or follow sports, I've never even seen him with a woman – all he's got are those dogs. If you killed Ace, he's going to kill you, it's as simple as that."

Dave couldn't doubt Pete's sincerity, but he couldn't believe him either. Instead of scaring him, the picture that emerged of the eccentric recluse touched him. Knowing that he'd killed an extraordinary dog, the pride and joy of an unloved misfit, intensified the guilt he already felt. He had to claim responsibility for what he'd done and try to atone for it. Maybe – no, he couldn't give him Rags, Carol and Alice would never stand for that, but he could offer to buy him another dog. Buster probably couldn't afford to buy a purebred Labrador.

"Where'd he get a dog like that in the first place?" he asked.

Pete now seemed reserved and wary. He had moved down the bar as if he feared he might get contaminated from closer contact with Dave and he was busying himself polishing glasses.

"Summer people left him behind, I suppose," he said after a pause. "I'm not sure about Ace, but that's how he got Trooper. Or else he stole him. He just naturally assumes that laws are made for other people. If he wants to do something, he goes ahead and does it."

Dave managed a smile. That's how he'd sized Buster up on the basis of their one encounter. He found the trait just a little bit enviable.

This time Pete didn't jump to refill his empty glass. Dave studied the bottles behind the bar and examined the rough-hewn beams of the ceiling for a while before asking, "Where does he live?"

"You'll regret it, I'm telling you."

"Come on, Pete, this isn't the Wild West."

Pete came back and looked at him without much warmth as he said, "I can give you the names of five guys he's beaten within an inch of their lives. For nothing at all, just because they looked at him the wrong way or made some perfectly harmless remark. He served time for punching out an officer when he was in the Army. There are also a few people that Buster didn't like who haven't been heard from lately, but I can't swear to anything there. No, Dave, this isn't the Wild West, but you have to take into consideration the fact that Buster doesn't know it."

Dave was beginning to doubt the wisdom of his own idea, but the idea itself had assumed a new dimension: it had become a challenge. If he took Pete's advice, if he went home now and hid the dog's collar, he would never be able to rid himself of the taste of his guilty secret. Maybe he should go home first and get his gun – but that thought was so absurd that it made his fears seem absurd, too.

"I think I have a responsibility to tell him about his dog. I'm not going to sneak out of it. Now, where does he live?"

"Go down the road here about two miles, take the first right. Just beyond a bridge, you'll find a miniature junkyard with a slapdash house behind it. That's him. The name's out front."

"Thanks."

"Look, why don't you have another beer? Think

about your wife and kids. Is it worth it, messing around with some wild man, all because of a no-good dog that got just what he deserved? It's stupid, that's what it is, just plain stupid."

Chapter Nine

The closer he got to Buster Callan's house, the more Dave was inclined to agree with Pete's opinion of his errand. None of the lines that he tried to compose for himself seemed playable, nor could he imagine Buster's reaction to any of them. If Pete was right about Buster, his reply to anything Dave might say would be a fist in the mouth, but he still thought that unlikely. He hadn't even seen a fistfight since high school, much less been involved in one. He believed that he was intelligent and articulate enough to talk his way out of a physical showdown. After all, his intention was to offer his apologies and some form of compensation for the dead dog, not to go a few rounds with its owner.

Anyway, Pete's evidence that Buster was a homicidal maniac hadn't been convincing. It had all sounded like hearsay and back fence gossip, particularly the part about the mysterious disappearances. Maybe Buster had reinforced those rumors once by throwing a bad scare into Pete during an argument over their business deals, whatever they might be.

Nevertheless, Dave began to hope that he wouldn't find Buster home. It seemed probable that he wouldn't.

Why would the wild man of the woods that Pete had described coop himself up in his house on such a fine afternoon? No doubt he would be out searching for his missing dog. The thought made him wince, and it strengthened his wavering resolution to carry out his unpleasant duty.

He turned off the main road and onto a graveled lane. The intermittent splashes of sunlight falling through the trees dazzled him. He was surprised to note his keen appreciation of the lovely day, of the damp spring breeze blowing off the woods. His worries were superficial, and he was neither frightened nor depressed by his mission. On the contrary, he had to admit that he was almost enjoying it. Doing anything – even this ghastly errand – that took him out of his study, that involved him in the unknown life of the countryside, was better than sitting home and tapping out unrealities on his typewriter.

This morning, checking through his notes for proposed projects, he came across one he had to write for a homemakers' magazine, creating attractive planters out of coffee cans with only a pair of tin snips. If the youth he had once been, the young Dave Stern who had dreamed of writing the Great American Novel, could have looked into the future and seen himself occupied with such inane hackwork – God only knows what he would have done. Shot himself, probably.

Maybe not. Owning a farm had always been his second ambition, and at least he'd achieved that much. Maybe his younger self would have forgiven the compromises he'd been forced to make.

He acknowledged that he was being much easier on himself than the younger Dave would have been. He wouldn't have accepted the word "compromise." He would have called it selling out, and he would have been right. Between the dream of the great novel and the reality – the sleazy magazine stories, the ghostwritten autobiography of a porno film actress, the half-witted do-it-yourself articles – there had been no common ground for compromise. He'd sold out, that was all there was to it, and he'd sold out cheap.

Nor had he achieved his second ambition, not really. He didn't own a farm, he owned a farmhouse surrounded by wasted land. He was no farmer, he was just another exurbanite dilettante. Somewhere along the line he had forgotten the purpose behind his ambition. He had wanted to lead a more honest life by getting back in touch with the rhythms of nature, by growing the food for his family with his own hands. He had wanted to show his children that meat didn't originate in plastic packages, that milk wasn't produced in cardboard cartons. His ambition had its roots in a youthful vision of the beauty of life in all of its organic symmetry, and he had lost touch with that vision.

He was suddenly struck by an idea that was simple and obvious, yet so far-reaching in its implications that it awed him: that it wasn't too late for him to get back in touch with the dreams of his youth and turn them into realities. If he could support his family by farming, he wouldn't have to write stupid articles about making planters out of coffee cans. He could write whatever he wanted to, without the necessity of keeping one eye constantly on the cash register.

It would mean a drastic change in their standard of living, of course, and the abandonment of many comfortable habits. He would no longer have the time or the money to spend in Pete's Tavern. Carol would have to give up her hopes for occasional junkets to New York. Alice would have to forget about her horse – no, not necessarily. A horse could pull a plough, and it would be cheaper and more in tune with nature than a tractor.

He would have to organize his thoughts and prepare to do some persuasive talking. Alice probably wouldn't need convincing. He knew that she believed in the same youthful ideals he'd once held. Mark – well, his strong back would have been an asset, but he didn't suppose Mark would stay with the family much longer. He was virtually an adult, with his own set of ambitions. Perhaps they weren't very lofty – to see the world and make a lot of money as a bulldozer jockey – but they were his, independently arrived at, and Dave respected them as such.

Carol. It was all up to her. She held the key to his future. If she disapproved of his idea, she could bring some powerful arguments to bear against it. She had invested all her money in their house on the assumption that he would continue to provide her with her accustomed standard of living. It would have been reasonable for her to suppose that his income would continue to rise. Now that she had burned her bridges behind her, he proposed to quit his job and gamble on a new career for which he was totally unprepared. Failure was almost a certainty, and success would be measured only in the inches they crawled above the poverty line. How could they meet the mortgage payments? They had paid $80,000 for a charming old house in a lovely setting; its potential as a productive farm was probably worth only a quarter of that amount.

He didn't have a rebuttal for those arguments. He would have to plan one before he even suggested his idea to her.

Gripped with enthusiasm for his new idea, he drove past Buster's house before the name on the sign registered. He braked sharply and pulled back to read it again: W.H. CALLAN, HUNTING AND FISHING GUIDE. The place looked even more run-down and depressing than Pete had suggested.

He lit a cigarette and tried to reorder his thoughts. His errand, all-important just a few minutes ago, now seemed a trivial nuisance. Get it over with, that was the only thing for him to do, then return to his serious thinking with a clear conscience. He hoped now that Buster would be home. It would be far harder on his nerves to leave a note and wait for Buster to get in touch with him than it would be to face him, tell him the truth, and witness his reaction.

He turned the car into the driveway and drove quickly up to the disorderly yard. The German shepherd began barking at him. He was indeed a monster. Fortunately the chain that held him to the porch looked heavy enough to support the anchor of a battleship, and it wasn't long enough for him to reach the steps. A line from an old Scots ballad – a ballad about a poacher – came unbidden to his mind: "Gie to me my twa great hounds, that lie bound in iron chains." Buster was certainly upholding the tradition.

Life was odd. If his plan succeeded, he would become like Buster Callan in many ways. He would have to repair his own machinery, as Buster obviously did. He would have to live off the land, just like Buster, hunting and fishing to supplement the food he could grow. Buster could teach him a lot, if – he laughed as he remembered again why he was here. Whatever the result of this encounter might be, it wouldn't make Buster his helpful friend.

He took Ace's collar from his glove compartment and slipped it into his pocket. He didn't want Buster to spot it in his hand before he spoke a word, even though he didn't yet know what that word should be.

He kept to the far edge of the steps as he climbed them. Storm Trooper sprang, ignoring his chain, and was caught short and flung on his back. That didn't improve his disposition.

The screen door rattled loosely as he knocked. It wasn't hooked. That might mean Buster was home, but not necessarily. More than once he had heard the boast that nobody ever locked his doors around here. He and Carol always did; though.

He shaded his eyes to probe the dim interior through the screen. He got only an impression of a dark room cluttered with massive Victorian furniture. Then he saw movement. He stepped back from the door.

Buster stepped onto the porch. He wore only a pair of faded jeans, and he now adjusted them on his wolfish hips as if he'd only just put them on. His dirty-blond hair was tousled. Dave hoped he hadn't awakened him. It hadn't occurred to him that a poacher probably , worked at night.

"Shut up, Troop," he called. There was no hint of recognition in his pale blue eyes as he turned them on Dave. "Yeah?"

"My name's Dave Stern, Mr. Callan. We met the other day, sort of, at Pete's place."

There was no hostility in his look. There was nothing in it. He seemed to be staring through Dave's head and focusing on a point ten feet beyond it.

"Yeah?" he repeated.

Dave wondered if he should offer to shake hands. He decided that should have been Buster's choice. Anyway, it was too late now to make the move.

"Well, this isn't a very pleasant . . . ah . . . thing for me to have to tell you. I'm afraid I've got some bad news for you. I shot your dog."

"You shot Ace, huh?"

Dave was astounded. He detected not even a flicker of surprise on Buster's face, not even a subtle alteration in his level tone of voice.

The silence stretched out. Dave felt sweat trickling down his neck. Then Buster asked, "Is he dead?"

Dave's hand behaved as if it were someone else's, and it took him a moment to fish the collar out of his pocket. He handed it to Buster. The sight of the bloodstains didn't seem to affect him.

"I'm sorry. Really. I love dogs. I have a dog of my own, and I heard that yours was an exceptional animal. It was an accident. Ace and some other dogs were running down a deer near my house. I wanted to shoot the deer and put it out of its misery, but my first shot missed and hit Ace. I'm sorry."

For the first time, Buster looked away. He scratched his hairless chest and stared down at his bare toes. Dave could see how he might be a dangerous opponent in a fight. He was five or six inches shorter than Dave, but his body was muscular and seemed utterly without fat. His scarred and calloused hands looked disproportionately large.

"Well," he said at last, and his lips twitched in a sort of stillborn smile, "I got some bad news for you, too, Jewboy. You're dead."

Buster's empty gaze was almost hypnotic. Dave found himself staring back, unspeaking, for a long time. He coughed, looked away, and said, "It was an accident, as I said. I guess you've got a right to be mad about it. I'd be mad, too. But I'm willing to make it up to you. I'll get you another dog, or pay you whatever you think Ace was worth."

Buster shook his head, and he actually smiled. "You got it wrong. I don't want your shekels. I want your blood."

"Wait –" Dave began, not knowing how to complete the sentence, as Buster turned and walked back into the house.

He waited on the porch for a minute or so, and then exasperation flooded him. He had wasted enough time on this nasty little redneck. He turned and sidled down the steps, well out of range of the snarling shepherd, and went to his car. Just as he touched the handle of the car door, he heard the screen door slam in back of him.

"Don't go away," Buster called in a pleasant voice.

Dave looked over his shoulder. Buster was coming down the steps with a double-barreled shotgun hooked over his forearm. He was trying to fit a shell into the breech. For the first time he revealed the depth of his emotions. His hand shook so badly that he couldn't load the gun.

Even though he couldn't believe it, Dave told himself that he was about to die. His knees must have believed it, because they began to tremble. But fear wasn't his predominant emotion. He was angry, outraged by the stupidity and injustice and wastefulness of what was going to happen.

"Buster, for Christ's sake – it was an accident! It was only a goddamned dog!"

Buster managed to thrust one shell and then the other into the breech of the shotgun. The gun clunked shut.

"People know where I am – they –"

A naked woman flung herself out of the house and tackled Buster from behind. She knocked him sprawling in the dirt. The shotgun flew from his hands. Dave took a step toward it.

"Run!" she screamed. "Get out of here! He'll kill you, mister. Get in your car and *go!*"

Buster rolled over on his back and tried to shove the woman away from him, but she hung on with savage determination. Even though he roared and cursed like a man in a mindless rage, he was obviously restraining himself from hurting her. He could have freed himself with one solid blow, but he didn't strike it. Each time he pried her hands loose, she would seize a fresh grip, and he would be forced to begin his efforts to get loose all over again.

The dog, meanwhile, was working itself into a frenzy as it snarled and barked and hurled itself against the limits of its chain. Dave watched, fascinated by the barbaric strangeness of the scene. Allowing for anachronistic touches like the woman's baroque hairstyle, he might have been witnessing a domestic squabble in front of a Neolithic cave.

"Get moving!" the woman screamed. "You want to get yourself killed?"

For just an instant he looked into her dark eyes, and he felt a chill of recognition. She was Pete's wife, Peggy. He struggled to keep from bursting into laughter as an old cliché crossed his mind: he hadn't recognized her without her uniform.

The spell that had held him frozen was broken now. He yanked the car door open and slid behind the steering wheel. He backed and turned and braked violently, stalling the car. He refused to look back as he cursed the grinding ignition. He was sure that Buster must be loose by now.

The engine caught, and he tore down the driveway. He was acutely conscious of the spot between his shoulder blades where he expected the blast to hit him. It didn't come.

He braved a glance in the rear-view mirror as he reached the gravel road, and what he saw made him hit the brake and stare back for a moment. Buster had forgotten all about him. On the hard-packed earth of his dooryard, he and Peggy were making love.

Chapter Ten

Carol ran to the phone when it rang, eager for any distraction. Halfway there, it occurred to her that it might be trouble. Dave had ignored her appeals to common sense, and this call would probably be from him – in some hospital.

Her voice was wary, "Hello?"

"Hi."

She gripped the receiver tightly. She said nothing as she yearned for the force of will necessary to hang up on Jack Prewitt.

"Carol? What's wrong, Carol?"

She couldn't hang up. She tried the next best thing, scolding him, but her tone didn't sound at all scolding as she said, "Jack – you shouldn't call me . . ."

"I wanted to talk to you. I had to hear your voice. Can you talk?"

She wanted to hear his voice, too. She gave up trying to resist. Laughing, she said, "Yes, I can talk. He's out. He shot somebody's dog, and he's off looking for the owner."

The moment of silence that followed made her realize how bizarre that must have sounded to Jack, calling as he was from the heart of civilization.

"You're kidding," he said with an uncertain laugh. "What's that all about?"

"Didn't you know? I'm the frail, consumptive beauty being held captive by the mysterious master of Ravenswood Manor, who spends his days shooting dogs and flogging peasants."

"Say no more, fair damsel, I'll come and rescue you."

It pleased her that he had joined her game and picked up his cue so quickly. Without thinking, she said, "I almost wish you would."

"I will. Can I see you this weekend? I'll drive up."

She was shocked. He meant it.

"No, no, no, absolutely not!" she said. "It's impossible."

"No, it isn't, I –"

"Not up here, really," she interrupted. "I couldn't get away from the house."

"Why bother?" he said. "I'll come there, right to your house, and we'll tell him."

"We have nothing to tell him, Jack. Don't be dumb."

"Yes, we do. We'll tell him that we love each other. We'll tell him that you're coming back to live with me."

"The children –"

"Are grown-up. You have no excuse on earth for not coming back here, for not doing what you want to do, for not being with me all the time."

Confused, frustrated, she vented her anger on Jack. "He has more money than you do," she snapped. "Be realistic."

She regretted her words as soon as they came out, but fortunately he chose to take them lightly. "I'll become a rock star, or a bank robber, or a tennis pro. All I need is your inspiration. And what good is money, if he uses it to drag you off to East Armpit Junction? Don't you want to come back?"

"I will. But for a week, or a few days."

"When?"

"I don't *know* when. I'm trying, really, I –"

She cut her words short. Before this, visiting Jack in the city had been only a vague notion, a daydream to preserve her sanity and a way of fending him off. It had suddenly become a certainty, a promise. She would go back – for a week, anyway.

"When?" he persisted.

"It's not easy. He's got the idea now that we'll *all* go when the school year ends. I'll talk him out of that, though, really I will. I'll –"

"Next week," he said.

"No, not next week, that's impossible –"

"Next week. Say it. Otherwise, you'll never do it."

She squeezed her eyes shut. "All right," she said, almost whispering, "next week."

"I love you, Carol," he said, and then he shocked her again by hanging up, not waiting for her to dictate a response.

She lowered the receiver to its cradle. He had never been so forceful, so insistent. Somehow he must have known that he was dealing from a position of strength, that she wouldn't be able to refuse him. Maybe he was smarter than she thought. Maybe he had calculated just how long it would take for this Green Mountain idyll to transform her into a sniveling wreck, begging for a chance to run back into his arms. Whatever the reason, she was no longer dealing with an innocuous pup. She was being told what to do – no, she was being told what she *wanted* to do.

He couldn't have picked a more perfect time to call, she reflected as she wandered back into the living room. Perversely, she had been doing something guaranteed to blacken her outlook on life: wading through all the copies of *New York Magazine* that she'd been tossing unread into a large wicker basket as soon as they arrived, the same basket that held Dave's unread copies of *Country Journal.* Skimming through the pages devoted to chic restaurants and trendy boutiques, to quests for the best pastrami or pizza or *dim sum,* to all the quirky luxuries available to New Yorkers, she had been consumed by pangs of envy and nostalgia.

She was gathering up the magazines when Rags began to give his welcoming barks, and a moment later she heard the car. She caught herself giving the room a guilty survey. But of course, there could be no telltale evidence of an unfaithful phone call. Except, perhaps on her face. It took some effort to compose it, but Dave hardly looked at her as he walked through to the kitchen. She heard the rattle of ice cubes.

"I'll have one, too," she called, following him. "Did you find the bereaved owner?"

He turned to look at her with an unfamiliar expression. He was smiling, but he looked shaken and bemused. The expression wouldn't have been inappropriate for the sole survivor of a plane crash. It was impossible, of course, but something inside her screamed that he had found out about Jack.

"Did you find the dog's owner?" she repeated, taking the stiff drink he handed her.

"Yeah. Now all I have to worry about is him finding me," he said.

He gave her a brief character sketch of Buster Callan and told her what had happened up to the point where Buster had come out of his house with the shotgun.

As he finished the story and sipped his drink, she inwardly cursed his fondness for theatrics. "So then he shot you, right?" she said, and her voice held more sarcasm than she had intended. "When do you fall down?"

"He was going to, believe me. He was absolutely shaking with rage. But at that point the cavalry came over the hill, in the form of a stark-naked woman who ran out of the house and knocked him flat on his face.

It was the damnedest thing! It was Pete Jensen's wife, and Pete had just been telling me how Buster never messed around with girls."

He topped off his drink from the bottle and sat down at the kitchen table. Carol felt like sitting down, too, but she leaned casually against the refrigerator.

"Peggy wasn't doing it for my sake, of course," he said. "It must have taken a lot of nerve to show herself like that – no, I didn't mean that pun, honest – but she was willing to give herself away in order to save Buster from twenty years on the rock pile."

"Have you called the police?"

Her question appeared to startle him. He hesitated, as if considering that course of action for the first time, and then said, "I'm sure that's the end of it. He's thrown a scare into me, chased me off his property – and shown off for his girl, too, maybe that was the point of it all. He's probably calmed down by now. As a matter of fact, wait till you hear the punch line –"

"What if he doesn't calm down?" she interrupted, irked by his assumption – so typical of him – that the world was full of easy-going, unrevengeful people like himself. "Hasn't he proved what Pete told you, that he's a bloodthirsty maniac? Hasn't he threatened your life? You've got to call the police."

He went through the repertoire of time-killing gestures – stroking his chin, staring out the window, making a clumsy production of lighting a cigarette – whose awkward transparency she had once thought charming. She now wondered why.

"Well?" she said.

"It would be my word against his," he said at last, "unless I tried to drag Peggy into it, and that would only serve to hurt her and Pete. And, probably, get old Buster even madder at me. And what do you suppose she'd say? Whatever Buster told her to say, of course."

She knew he was right, but she refused to accept the

fact that they were helpless to do anything but wait for Buster's next move. She knew that he would make one. All the menace of the evil old hills, the hostile stares in the supermarket, the nasty secrets guarded in the isolated farmhouses – all of her unformed fears had found a focus in the horrid little man whom Dave had described. Dave had brought the wrath of the land itself down upon their heads.

Just as there was a bit of Sally Fudd in her husband, so was there a frustrated streak of Rob Masterman – his unexpected competence with tools and with that damned gun, his ability to protect them during the power failure, and now his priggishly old-fashioned rectitude. He had gone to Buster Callan like a Boy Scout bravely owning up to a broken window – unaware that he was facing an avatar of all the ancient, dangerous things that lurked beyond the firelight of the home cave – and now he was hurt that Buster hadn't offered him milk and cookies.

She sat down at the table opposite him, unwilling to put her deepest fears into words. Maybe she was letting her imagination run wild. She didn't think so. She and Dave didn't belong here, and some drastic proof of that had been long overdue. Without even knowing about Buster Callan, she had been expecting him to turn up.

She saw that Dave was studying her with a puzzled look. She tried to seem attentive, interested in the rest of his story.

"So what was that about a punch line?"

He laughed. "So here I was, tearing down his driveway, expecting a load of buckshot at any second, when I looked back and saw that I was the last thing on his mind. He was screwing her, right out in the front yard."

She shuddered. She couldn't share Dave's laughter. She didn't know why, but that touch made the episode even more sinister.

"Funny about her," he said, not noticing her reaction. "I've seen her a dozen times, maybe, and I never gave her a second look. Sort of big and ungainly, that's the impression I had, maybe pretty in a cheap kind of way. When I saw her today, I didn't even recognize her at first. She's one of those women who look a hundred percent better with their clothes off."

She couldn't resist saying, "I didn't know you were such an expert."

"Well, you know what I mean," he hurried to say. His obvious embarrassment delighted her. She felt a sudden resurgence of affection for him. "Like fashion models and figure models, you know, some women look good in clothes and some – I mean. . . ."

"I know what you mean," she laughed, reaching out to take his hand.

He squeezed her hand and became more serious. "It's a lousy thing. Now it would be awkward for me to go back to my favorite bar. Not just because I'd run into Peggy, but because I'd have trouble looking Pete in the eye, knowing what I know."

The temptation was strong to tell him that the bar's loss was his gain, but she succeeded in beating down the impulse.

"Pete's a decent sort of guy," he said. "And this Buster – I think I've been inclined to romanticize my idea of him, because he's so well-adapted to his environment, because he's capable and tough enough to squeeze a living out of impossible surroundings. But you could say the same thing about a mugger in the city. But you don't look at a mugger with the same set of literary allusions, going all the way back to the old border ballads. A poacher and a mugger are both crooks, but the poacher has the advantage of operating out of prettier scenery."

"That's not the only difference," she said dryly. "Shooting a deer out of season isn't quite the same thing as knocking an old lady over the head and swiping her purse."

"It's only a question of opportunity. If there were old ladies with purses wandering around in the woods, Buster would probably be knocking them over the head. If he lived in the city he'd adapt to that sort of life. It's not at all hard to picture him as a member of some neo-Nazi motorcycle gang in Queens. He's got all the right attitudes. He's got it into his head that I'm a Jew, and I think that bothers him almost as much as the fact that I shot his dog."

"Did you try telling him that you aren't?"

An expression of annoyance passed over his face, but he softened it by giving her hand another squeeze. "I've been doing that all my life. I've done it too often. Correcting people who jump to that conclusion – it's the same thing as saying, 'Look, I'm a member of the club, too, you can make all the bigoted remarks you want.'"

It galled her that she couldn't find fault with his moral position. He seemed determined to achieve sainthood today, to turn himself into an insufferable prig. After dinner, maybe, he would go out and look for a couple of lepers to kiss. She turned her head away, fighting the giggle that was on the verge of bursting forth.

"Seeing something like that – it really made me feel, I don't know, sad, sort of, but grateful at the same time," he said.

His tone – he sounded as if he were choked with emotion – startled her, forcing her to look at him.

"What are you talking about?" she asked.

"Pete and Peggy. Here's this guy who's absolutely crazy about his wife, you can see it in every look he gives her, every word he speaks to her. He's proud of her, too, even though she's . . . well, I shouldn't say anything, but I guess she could be described as ordinary, in regard to brains and personality. Anyway, he's crazy about her, but he must not understand her at all or be able to achieve any communication with her. I'm certain he has no idea of what she's doing behind his back."

"So?"

"So what I'm saying is, it makes me – grateful that we've got each other. It makes me appreciate how much we understand each other, how deeply we can communicate. Sometimes I feel so close to you that – that it's as if we were one person."

She couldn't bring herself to meet his earnest gaze. Her hand still lay in his grasp. She wished she could think of a way to withdraw it without making that seem a comment on his words.

Chapter Eleven

It was a good thing she liked corned beef hash with eggs poached on top of it, Alice reflected, because they got it often enough for dinner. Lately she had been working out a theory, that Mom cooked an egg dish for dinner when she was angry with Dad. Like omelets and soufflés, hash with eggs tended to show up when the tension between them was running high. She believed that her theory allowed her even to gauge the degree of Mom's irritation. Since soufflés took the most trouble, she would cook those when she was mildly annoyed; omelets, less difficult to prepare, indicated a deeper grievance; but hash with eggs, no trouble at all, was a warning that an explosion was imminent.

Tonight her theory suffered a setback. Mom was quiet, but she seemed relaxed. She wasn't even picking on Mark, and that was how she usually warmed up for the main event with Dad. Mark regarded meals as pit stops in his race with time. He would keep his head down and shovel in the food, grunting in response to any question that couldn't simply be ignored, then tear out of the house before anyone else had really started in on the meal. On those unpleasant egg-nights, Mom's voice would sound affected; her diction would be overprecise as she asked Mark searching questions about his school work or his love life or about the state of the world in general. If he turned out to be less clever and articulate in his answers than Oscar Wilde, she would fly into a snit. She would make him sit at the table and fidget with his empty plate while she complained to Dad about his bad manners.

Starting with the eggs, Alice believed, the whole performance was meant to be a protest against the fact that they were no longer living in the city. It was Mom's way of saying that eggs from their own backyard were the only decent things they had to eat, because she couldn't get escargot or calf's brains or shad roe in Lettie Miller's general store; and it was also her way of saying that Mark was a morose lout because he was going to a third-rate school with a bunch of future farmers. Even before they'd moved to Vermont she'd picked on Mark for being a morose lout – since he was – and they had eaten egg dishes for dinner often enough in New York, but Mom colored everything she did up here with new shades of resentment.

As if to prove Alice right in her assessment of him, Mark mumbled, "What's this crap in the salad?"

"Those are dandelion greens, dear," Carol said, with just a hint of that special tone of precision in her voice. "Alice picked them this afternoon."

"No, I mean this other crap."

"Knock it off, Mark," Dad said without much heat.

"Those are scallions," Mom said.

"Same source, huh?" Mark said, and he shot Alice a sneering smile. "Sheesh."

Alice refused to rise to the bait or even look at him. She was going to get a horse, and she wasn't going to blow that by being anything less than a perfect little lady until she had her hands on it.

"That's pretty clever," Dad said, obviously pleased. "Where'd you get the idea?"

"Euell Gibbons," she said, smiling back. That was a book he'd given her last Christmas: *Stalking the Wild Asparagus.* She hadn't found any wild asparagus yet, even though she kept looking.

"There's lots of things we could do like that to put a little, uh, more variety in our lives," Dad said. "Not only would we be having fun, but we'd also be economizing a little bit by living off the land."

That was one of Dad's favorite topics. Mark and Mom looked at their food, but Alice looked at him attentively, as if hearing it all for the first time. He deserved more encouragement than he got around here, and she tried her best to give him some.

"I ought to grow some things, too. I was just thinking that today," he said. "As it is, we've got a lot of land just going to waste. And the chickens have been pretty successful."

"Yeah, they all drive around in Cadillacs," Mark said, and everyone laughed – not only because his comment was funny, but because he so seldom tried to make jokes at the table that it came as a mild shock.

Alice saw the laughter as a good opportunity to change the subject before Dad started boring everybody to death, so as it subsided, she asked, "Did you find the man whose dog you shot?"

"Yeah," he said, and she saw him exchange a glance with Mom. "He wasn't too happy about it."

"What did he say?" Mark asked.

This time Dad ignored Mom's look, which was obviously a warning, and said, "He said he was going to shoot me, and then he went and got his gun to do it."

"No!" Alice cried. "What happened?"

"Oh, nothing, really, he just chased me off his land. He was pretty upset at the moment, that's all."

"Who was it?" Mark asked.

"I don't think –" Mom started to say, but Dad overrode her. "Buster Callan."

"Oh, yeah." Mark laughed. "Some guys at school were talking about him – he's the local crazoid. He goes out in the woods naked, with a knife in his teeth, to kill bears."

Mom was getting steadily more displeased with the conversation, so Dad changed the subject. "Your mother and I were talking about going to New York for a week or so when school closes."

"But he only does that during blizzards, otherwise he thinks it's sissy stuff," Mark added, but this time he got no encouragement.

"When there's no school, that's the nicest time to be here," Alice said.

She thought she'd made merely a neutral observation – she wasn't opposed to going to the city – and so she was surprised when Mom picked her words up quickly, and with obvious pleasure.

"That's true, you know, Dave," she said. "Alice and Mark have been cooped up in school all this time, looking at the great outdoors without being able to enjoy it –"

"May I be excused?" Mark asked, knowing it was best to slip that request in when no one was paying him any attention.

Dad waved him away casually as he said, "But I thought you were the one who wanted to go.

"I do, but what's the point of dragging everyone else along if they're not keen on going?" Mom asked. "I could go next week – say, Tuesday or Wednesday. It wouldn't cost as much, and we wouldn't need to uproot everyone. Mark . . . where did Mark go?"

"I told him he could leave," Dad said.

"Well, anyway, you don't really want to go, do you?"

"No, I guess, not really," Dad said.

Alice methodically mixed the remainder of her hash

with her egg. It had become unappetizing.

"If we all went, we'd have to stay at a hotel, but I can stay with Paul and Helen if I go by myself," Mom said. "And I'd have more time to see all the friends who bore you, Cissy Parker and everybody. While I'm gone, Alice can try out all her Euell Gibbons recipes on you."

She added that with a bright smile at Alice, who winced at being brought forth as an argument for Mom's purpose.

"Shall I clean up the dishes?" Alice asked.

Nobody noticed her, so she got up and gathered the dishes and took them to the kitchen while her parents continued their conversation. She felt irritation simmering just beneath the surface of her composure. She'd thought that Mom had gotten over that jerk, Mr. Prewitt, but apparently she hadn't.

She scraped the remnants of the hash and salad into Rag's bowl, doing it noisily enough to arouse him. When he didn't come, she whistled, but that didn't bring him either. She began to wash the dishes.

It was hard to say when everything had come together in her head, when she had known just what was going on. They'd always been perfectly proper and detached from each other when she was around – a little too proper and detached, maybe. Mom had been acting strangely one summer, running off to the Village at the drop of a hat, coming home at all hours, but she hadn't suspected anything then. The strangest thing happened when Mom decided to transfer her to that dumb new school for no good reason.

The only pleasure that Alice had ever taken from school was in getting better grades than everybody else, and the Village Educational Collective didn't even give grades. The students were encouraged to express themselves, which they did by ignoring schoolwork and raising hell in class. They were mostly the spoiled children of people engaged in the arts, and the school was designed to spoil them even further. Alice loathed each and every minute of it.

At first she'd suspected that her English teacher, Mr. Prewitt, was another Humbert Humbert, he was so . . . so solicitous of her. It was as if he considered her the only person in the class worth noticing. All his lectures were delivered directly to her, as if they were engaged in private conversation. He would ask her five or six times during a class if she understood and appreciated what was going on. If she got her name right on a paper, he would give her a smile and a nod; greater achievements would send him sailing off into raptures of appreciation.

She found everything about him, especially all the attention he gave her, repellent. She began to spend the classes staring out the window and ignoring him, trying to be as rude as all the other kids. She hated doing that, even to Mr. Prewitt, and she almost pitied his desperate attempts to regain her attention. She had come to the conclusion that he wasn't after her bod, but there was something definitely wrong with his behavior.

It was then that Mom started coming in for special conferences, and she got the opportunity to' see them with each other. She began to suspect why Mom was taking the long, pointless trips to Balducci's all the time, and she was disgusted with herself for her evil suspicions. But when she found out that Mr. Prewitt had been Mom's tennis partner all of the previous summer – and recalled that she had never once mentioned his name, even though she was always chattering about Cissy and Brad – she could no longer deny those suspicions.

She returned to the dining room, where Mom was giggling and batting her eyelashes at Dad as they finished their wine. Alice guessed that the trip to New York was settled.

"Where's Rags?"

Mom looked for a moment as if she didn't recognize the name, then shrugged and said, "I don't know, I haven't seen him."

"I whistled and called him and all, and he just didn't come. Could he be outside, do you think?"

"Did anybody feed him?" Dad asked.

"Now that you mention it, no," Mom said. "He wasn't around when I was cooking supper, so I didn't think of it."

"I hope he didn't get some ideas from those dogs yesterday, and go off chasing a deer," Dad said.

"I'll go look for him." Alice turned and ran from the room.

She got the flashlight from the kitchen before going out into the yard. She called, but she got no response. She thought it far likelier that the dogs who had chased the deer yesterday had come back to chase Rags. Whether it was his instinct or not, she just couldn't see that big dummy in a predatory role. He might have been hurt in a fight and have dragged himself under the porch. To die, she positively refused to add, even though the words popped into her mind.

She crawled deep under the porch, waving the fan of light before her. Cobwebs brushed her face, but she fixed her mind firmly on what she was doing and ignored them. She found a Rags-sized hole, its sides tamped down and smoothed by much use. In it were some bones, the shreds of a tennis ball, and one of her Pumas that had mysteriously disappeared a month ago.

She called him and shone the light once more around the crawl space, but there were no other burrows.

Only when she was once more out in the open air and dusting off her jeans did she allow herself to think how brave she'd been about the spiders. But that seemed unimportant. Rags was still missing.

She walked down through the orchard. It was still daylight in the sky, but darkness had fallen here in the shadow of the mountain behind the house. She had to flash her light intermittently to make sure of her way. On a few recent occasions, Rags had been waiting for her at the mailbox when she came home from school. It was the furthest she'd known him to venture from the house, and it seemed logical that he would have gone in that direction. Maybe he'd followed Mark's car out the drive, hoping for a ride. He loved to ride in cars.

That didn't explain why he hadn't been home for supper. If she had been doing her job, if she'd called him to eat, his absence would have been noticed at least an hour ago. She'd fallen into the habit of letting Mom feed him, since he always showed up in the kitchen anyway when Mom started to cook. Tonight Mom hadn't noticed his absence, though, because tonight she'd had more important things on her mind. She couldn't tell who deserved more of the blame, herself or her mother.

Poor Daddy. He was so kind and generous and brilliant – well, no, he wasn't very brilliant about his own family. She was sure he didn't know a thing about Mom and Mr. Prewitt. And she herself could always get anything she wanted from him with the most transparent devices, like waiting for him to have a fight with Mom before asking him for a horse. She had known he would say yes, just for the sake of rattling Mom.

She felt guilty about that. Playing one parent against the other only made their problems worse. But she'd really wanted a horse. If she didn't find Rags – it took her a moment to work up enough courage to make the vow – if she didn't find Rags, she would tell Dad that she didn't deserve to have a horse. Maybe not tell him that she didn't want one, not exactly, but just say that she didn't deserve one. No, that was a cop-out. She made a firmer vow, that she would refuse to accept a horse if she didn't find Rags.

She remembered him under the Christmas tree with a red ribbon around his neck, a big-footed puppy with a wet tongue. She'd been eight, and she'd wanted a puppy as she'd never wanted anything before in her life –

She cut of those memories abruptly. This was no time to break down and start getting sloppy about Rags. She had to concentrate on finding him.

Mr. Prewitt. He had a silly little beard, and even though he wasn't nearly as old as Dad, he was already going bald. He had a round face, like a big zero, with no character in it. Character was supposed to come from suffering.

Maybe he'd get some of that if he hung out with Mom long enough.

Those thoughts weren't doing her any good either. She was helpless in that situation. Telling Dad was unthinkable – it would tear him up. Telling Mom anything was equally unthinkable. They just couldn't talk to each other outside the roles Mom had cast them in: Mom was the all-wise parent, and she was the innocent child. In the context of those roles, she just couldn't take her mother aside and say, "Look, Mom, you're really screwing up, sleeping with a pipsqueak like Mr. Prewitt –"

Mom wouldn't even *hear* her if she said that; she would pretend that something entirely different had been said. "Yes, dear, the forks are supposed to go on that side of the plate," Mom would answer. And she would say, "No, Mom, I mean cheating on a terrific guy like Dad with Mr. Prewitt, that's *sick!*" And Mom would say, "You ought to be more polite to Mr. Prewitt, Alice, rudeness just isn't your style." And she –

She screamed as she walked into a soft, heavy object.

It moved away from her. Then, as she stood frozen with fear, it returned and bumped against her.

She sprang back and flashed on the light. She had bumped into Rags. He had been hanged by the neck from the bough of an apple tree.

Chapter Twelve

Dave had always been lulled to sleep before by the creaking of the house as it settled further into its ancient foundations, the chirping of the crickets, the occasional sleepy clucking of the hens, but not tonight. His ears tried to sift out alien sounds from the familiar chorus. He kept imagining that he heard them.

He looked at Carol, her face a pale blur against the pillow. She seemed to be asleep. He wished that she were awake. A few years ago, he would have awakened her, and she wouldn't have minded. Now—well, maybe she still wouldn't object, maybe she would understand his need to talk to her, to hold her in his arms, to be comforted. It was a selfish desire, and he didn't give in to it.

He eased his legs out of bed and found the bottoms of his pajamas with his feet. He slid into them and padded quietly from the room. Maybe a drink would help.

He hesitated at the door of Alice's bedroom, wondering if he should look in on her. Probably not. He might wake her, and she certainly needed her sleep. Last night he'd sat beside her bed, trying to comfort her with his presence, until she'd finally dropped off at four. Then she'd gone to school this morning, despite his urging her to stay home. She had to do something, she said, anything except sit around the house all day and think about Rags.

Her decision was sensible, but he'd worried about her. A kid was singularly defenseless and uncomprehending in the face of wanton cruelty, but even so, her reaction to it had seemed disproportionate. "Life is so rotten, Daddy," she sobbed, "I just don't want to be alive anymore!" She sounded like she meant it, and she didn't normally indulge in that sort of verbal extremism.

He went on down the stairs and into the kitchen, where the glare of the overhead light made his eyes ache. Carol almost never used it, claiming that overhead lights made everything look ghastly. He had to admit she was right. The ghastliest thing of all was his own reflection in the black window over the sink. He turned it off as soon as he'd switched on the table lamp.

The state troopers had showed up at mid morning to confirm his belief that there wasn't much they could do. As he'd tried to explain to Carol, you don't look for footprints in a grassy orchard; nor do you find fingerprints on tree bark, rope, or a dog's hide. Buster had left no melodramatic note, nothing at all to claim his handiwork. Assuming, of course, that it had indeed been Buster. He knew in his guts that Buster killed Rags, but it could just as easily have been some other nut who didn't like their dog.

The policemen had been more interested in the details of his confrontation with Buster. They jotted down Dave's recollections of the threats that had been uttered; they asked if the gun had been fired. And, of course, they asked if there had been any witnesses. Carol had opened her mouth at that point, but fortunately she had had second thoughts and shut it. He told the police that he and Buster had been alone.

They said they would talk to Buster. They knew him from way back, they said, although they didn't go into the details of that acquaintanceship.

Now as he sipped his drink, it occurred to him that having the police talk to Buster might be worse than doing nothing. It would merely prove to Buster that he'd scored, that the city slickers were running in circles and wringing their hands and screaming for the cops. Buster would know as well as he did that the police were impotent in a situation like this. He would just get a good laugh out of it. Worse, it might encourage him to do something more.

He'd postponed Rags's burial until the police had seen him. Cops had to deal with all sorts of screwballs, and he wanted to make sure they knew that there really had been a dog, that he really had been strangled.

Later, spading the earth into the shallow grave behind the henhouse, he had remembered that famous exchange from a Sherlock Holmes story. Holmes refers to "the curious incident of the dog in the nighttime." When reminded that the dog did nothing at all during the nighttime, Holmes replies, "That was the curious incident."

It was damned curious. Why hadn't Rags barked? No matter how much of a genius Buster was with dogs, he couldn't have approached the house without being challenged by a paranoid like Rags. The alternative, that he was so skillful a hunter that he could creep up on dogs unnoticed, was chilling.

On a hunch, Dave had gone across the weir to the other grave he'd dug so recently and found the apparent answer. A dog – Rags, no doubt – had made a determined but unsuccessful attempt to dig up the stag. Buster must have approached the house from the woods beyond the pond and come upon Rags there. Rags might have barked, but they probably wouldn't have noticed the distant sound from inside the house.

Suppose Buster had come upon Alice first, instead of Rags . . .

That line of thought was unprofitable, to say the least. He had to assume that Buster had come here to kill the dog: Dave had mentioned to him that he owned a dog, and he had come to exact an eye for an eye. Now his vengeance was complete. It was all over.

He refilled his glass and went to his study. He still wasn't sleepy. If anything, his recollections of the trying day had left him even more wide-awake. He had been making an effort to keep more normal hours lately, but this looked like it was going to be a white night. He might as well try to do some work.

He had just seated himself at his typewriter when an uproar burst upon his ears. It took him a moment to identify the source of the noise as the chickens. He wouldn't have believed them capable of making such a sudden and concerted explosion of sound.

He ran through to the back porch and flung open the door. Some animal must have been raiding the henhouse, a fox or a weasel. Then he heard growling. It was loud even over the clamor of the frantic chickens, the growling of a huge dog, occasionally muffled as it shook and tore its prey. He snapped on the backyard light and tried to remember where he'd put his rifle to keep it out of Carol's way.

"Hi, Dave."

The soft sound of the man's voice made him cry out with shock. He saw a small man standing in the shadows. He saw the gleam of a gun barrel. The gun was raised. Light tore the darkness open; a crash of sound deafened him.

He hit the floor. He thought he'd been shot, but his fall had been an instinctive reaction. He saw that a chunk of the doorframe above him had been blown away. A second shot sounded, and the outdoor light went out. He scrambled back into the house.

Staying on the floor, he pulled the plug of the table lamp. He heard more shots, but Buster was no longer firing at the house. He was blasting away at the henhouse, helping his dog finish off the chickens.

He got up and ran to the study, where he had put the gun. He was ramming shells into the magazine when Carol appeared and grabbed his arm.

"What, what? What's happening? What is it?" she demanded.

"Buster."

"I'll call the police."

"Don't call the police," he said, pushing her back toward the study as he left. "No, don't call the police, not unless you want me arrested for murder. I'm going to kill that son-of-a-bitch."

"Dave!" she screamed after him, but her words couldn't be heard over the roaring inside his head.

He heard a car starting at the foot of the driveway as he reached the door. The backyard was absolutely silent. Buster must have killed every last one of them. He turned back and snatched his jacket from a peg by the door. He slipped it on over his pajamas and fumbled in the pockets until he was sure he had the keys to the station wagon.

"Where are you going, Dave? For God's sake, what do you think you're doing?" Carol shouted, clutching at his arm.

He shook her off. "I told you what I'm doing."

"You're crazy! Do you hear me? You're insane!"

The wagon seemed airborne most of the time as he roared down the uneven driveway. His head hit the ceiling each time it crashed down on its springs. The rear end swung around as he turned into the dirt road, but he steered into the skid without slowing down and righted the car. The needle of the speedometer hit eighty before he reached the paved road. The tires shrieked as he skidded into another turn on the macadam. He saw taillights ahead of him.

The car was an extension of his rage; he didn't drive it by thought. He was incapable of thought. The two red eyes ahead of him were everything. He was joined to them, drawn to them as if by a strand of steel. They were getting bigger.

He remembered to turn on the headlights, and that action seemed to signal the return of human consciousness. The lights showed him the scrapes and rust-pits on the trunk of Buster's old Chevrolet. The trunk seemed to be rushing toward him, but then it suddenly began to pull away. He jammed his foot down until he was standing on the accelerator, but Buster's car kept drawing away from him.

Dave began to shake. He slumped back into the seat, easing the pressure on the accelerator. He looked at the speedometer: 110. He slowed even more, all the way down to 70. He seemed to be crawling at that speed. The taillights disappeared around a bend.

He glanced into the lot at Pete's Tavern as he passed it. The lot was crowded, but Buster's battered heap stood out. Dave braked and swung in behind it. He got out of his car. He reached back for his rifle, but taking it suddenly seemed like a very foolish thing to do. His hand lingered on the stock for a moment before he decided not to take it.

As he stood up and slammed the door, he saw Buster leaning against his own car. He wasn't carrying his shotgun, and his dog was in the car. Buster was smiling.

"You're one hell of a driver," Buster said. "You scared the living shit out of me when you turned on your headlights."

Dave walked toward him, his fists clenched at his

sides. It surprised him to realize the depth of his own fear, but he wouldn't back down.

"We have to settle this," Dave said.

Buster pushed himself away from his car and shrugged. "It's settled, as far as I'm concerned. No, I'm wrong, I owe you one. Killing your goddamn chickens, that was a candy-ass thing to do. I'm sorry I did it."

Dave stopped. "You rotten son-of-a-bitch," he said, "I . . ."

"If you want to hit me, go ahead. Like I said, I owe you one."

Dave put his hands down on the trunk of Buster's car and leaned heavily on them, staring at the faded green paint.

"You won't even understand this, you bastard. That's the worst part of it. You killed my daughter's dog. She never hurt a living creature in her life – if she finds an ant in the house she picks it up and carries it outside. And you damned near drove her crazy with grief."

"You told me it was your dog."

Dave looked away and rubbed his nose. His eyes were misting over. Even he didn't understand what he was trying to say, never mind Buster.

"I would have given you that dog," Dave went on. "My daughter would have given him to you. We – I never killed anything, either. I didn't mean to kill Ace. I told you that."

"Maybe there's a couple of things you don't understand –"

"Shut up. My daughter got those ideas from me, about how life is sacred. Listen to me. I got arrested twice, I got roughed up by cops in Washington, because I protested against the Vietnam War. I nearly lost a job on account of my beliefs, but I couldn't be a silent party to murder. I've written articles and letters opposing the death penalty. Once I lost a good sale because I refused to put some graphic violence into a story I'd written. You don't agree with all that, I know."

"I never killed anything without a reason before. That's why –"

"Shut up. This is what I'm trying to tell you. I believe those things. I've tried to live by them, and I've succeeded. Up until tonight. Tonight you attacked my home. You endangered the lives of my wife and children, you slaughtered a lot of harmless, stupid chickens, you took a shot at me."

"If I mean to hit something, I –"

Trembling with rage, Dave turned to face him and took a step closer. The dog started barking, but Buster silenced him with a chopping gesture.

"Listen to me," Dave said. "You have to hear me out before I lose what it is I'm trying to say. Tonight you made me forget everything I believe in. I came after you to kill you, to put a bullet through your head – and if I'd caught up with you ten minutes earlier, by God, I would have done it! Do you understand? On top of everything else you've done to me, you've forced me to give up everything I held sacred. And that's, really . . . Christ, I still want to kill you for that."

"Well, shit, you sure sound confused. Why don't you come on inside and have a drink with me instead?"

Dave looked at him. It was impossible for him to tell what was on Buster's mind. But now that he had spent the last of his rage in words, the invitation was welcome.

"Like this?" he said, gesturing down at his pajamas, his bare feet.

"You're with me, nobody'll laugh. Anyway, we got our guns in the cars."

Buster seemed to be parodying himself, and it startled Dave to find he was capable of it. He laughed nervously.

"You're right," Buster continued, "I don't agree with your commie ideas, but I respect a man that has any kind of principles. I don't run into many. Come on."

He walked toward the bar without looking back. Dave found himself following. Inside it was dark and crowded enough for his outfit to go unnoticed. They sat at a table in a corner, and Buster ordered two beers from a waitress. He drank his beer in one gulp and banged the glass on the table for a refill before the waitress had gone three paces.

The girl, overworked and irritable, rounded on Buster. "If you're so goddamned thirsty, why didn't you order a pitcher in the first place? I can't keep running back to your table every minute. And if you're just going to drink beer, why don't you sit at the bar?"

Dave regretted having come. He expected a scene, probably a violent one, to erupt. Buster surprised him by answering the waitress mildly. "To tell you the truth, honey, I didn't even think of ordering a pitcher. Would you bring us one, please?"

As the waitress left, muttering, Buster said, "I want to tell you something, too. I went crazy when you killed my dog. When – I tried to shoot you the other day, that would have been the best way to settle it, because after that, thinking about Ace, I went clean out of my mind, and it scared me. Hanging your dog. Shit, I mean, that was insane. I should have shot you, or beat you up."

Dave sipped his beer and wondered what to say to that. He couldn't very well agree. He saw Pete behind the bar, his bald head gleaming with sweat, but he was too busy to notice them.

"Ace was . . . well, we used to do our thinking for each other. I can't explain that. We used to go up on Mount Easton together, just him and me, and it was like we were the only people – the only person – in the world. It looks like every other mountain around here, but it's a bastard to get up it, so you don't meet any sightseers or pussy hikers. He even saved my life once, from that other damned dog. You might just as well have blinded me, or cut off my right arm. An accident? Okay, okay, if I shot your daughter by accident, you wouldn't shake my hand and send me on my way, would you?"

"I don't know."

"Well, I didn't know either. I went and hung your dog. That was dumb. Then you sent the cops around to beat the shit out of me."

"I didn't –"

"Yeah, I suppose you couldn't know that, that they like to find excuses to bounce me around every so often. So I went and killed your chickens. That made me feel kind of sick with myself. It wasn't until I was driving away that it came over me what a white man you are. You could've dragged Peggy into it, and you didn't. So just as I was beginning to think I had you wrong, here you come trying to run me over, scaring me out of a year's growth. I never thought I would want to shake the hand of some . . . guy from New York City, but I would like to shake yours, mister."

"Try it more often," Dave said, gripping Buster's hard hand. "Maybe you'll find it doesn't hurt at all."

Chapter Thirteen

The sun was high when Carol opened her eyes. She couldn't at first account for its brightness. Jack's apartment, facing a back courtyard, was always gloomy and – no, that had been a dream. She felt a pang of loss and closed her eyes, trying to will herself back into the dream.

Full memory returned in the next instant. She sat up and stared at Dave beside her. He lay on his back, mouth open, snoring lightly. She grimaced at the sour odors of stale beer and male sweat.

She hadn't heard him come in. After calming down Mark and Alice as well as she could, she'd waited up as long as possible. The urge to call the police had been strong, but she'd resisted it. She'd had no doubt at all that Dave meant it when he said he was going to kill Buster; and despite the morality she'd always thought she believed in, it seemed like the only thing to do, the only way of protecting their home.

She hadn't been able to keep her eyes open. After dozing off twice, she'd stumbled to bed, filled with a sense of guilt for not being able to wait up for her husband, but unable to deny her body's need for sleep any longer.

And now here he was, just as he was every morning of her life. Could she have dreamed the whole thing? She had to work up her courage before nudging him. She wasn't sure she wanted to know what had happened.

"Mrf," he said, rolling away and trying to bury his head in the blankets.

"Dave, wake up!" she cried sharply as she shook his arm.

"Come on, what's the matter?" he mumbled. "What time is it?"

She found herself looking at the clock, abruptly remembering the children – but no, it wasn't a school day, it was Sunday. It was nearly eleven o'clock.

"What difference does it make, what time it is?" she almost screamed. "What happened? What did you do to him?"

"Oh." He rolled onto his back, rubbing his face. His smile appalled her. "Yeah, you mean Buster. It's okay. Everything's all right."

"I don't understand," she said slowly, unable to put the question directly. "What happened?"

"You mean, did I shoot him? Hell, no," he laughed. "I really acted like an idiot, didn't I? I don't know what came over me. Anyway, we both came to our senses. We shook hands and had a few beers at Pete's."

"I don't understand," she repeated, looking away from him. She felt an acute sense of – disappointment? It seemed a ghoulish reaction, but she couldn't help it, that was what she felt. She felt angry, too, very angry, even though her anger as yet had no precise focus. She jerked out of bed and busied herself with dressing. She avoided looking at her husband.

"I've never felt like that before," he said thoughtfully. "I could have killed him. I came that close to it. It scared me, feeling like that."

"Do you want breakfast?" She tried to keep her voice neutral, but she knew it sounded chilly.

"Yeah, I guess so." He hadn't noticed. "You know what –"

She fled from the bedroom before he could finish whatever it was he'd planned to say.

"Mom, is Daddy all right?"

Alice, sleepy-eyed, confronted her in her long nightgown.

"Did he –"

"He's just fine," Carol interrupted. "He made friends with the man who killed your dog. They're old drinking buddies now."

She didn't wait to watch her daughter's reaction but hurried down the stairs and into the kitchen. The infamous rifle was once again leaning by the door, dominating her kitchen with its malignant presence. She went through the small porch and examined the ragged gap in the doorframe, reassuring herself that she hadn't dreamed it all. Her eyes didn't linger on the welter of bloody chicken feathers in the run as she went back inside.

In her resentment and frustration, she felt exactly like the victim of a cruel and elaborate practical joke. Like a joker's butt, she had been set up. She had been led to believe that a man would be killed and that, by her inaction, she would be an accomplice in the murder. To accept that, she had been forced to perform radical surgery on her most basic emotions, on her deepest values, and the wounds still hurt.

And now the principal joker had whipped off his horrifying mask and expected her to laugh along with him.

She arranged bacon in the frying pan and set out four eggs. It occurred to her that they wouldn't have any more eggs, not unless she bought them at the market. The thought gave her a momentary flicker of pleasure that she suppressed irritably.

Dave came into the kitchen and inspected the coffee pot, even though it was obviously still perking. He was subdued now, and she knew he was studying her guardedly and trying to gauge her mood. Maybe Alice had said something to demolish his smug sense of accomplishment. She hoped so.

"The cops beat him up," he said.

"Who?"

"Buster. That's why he came back here last night. They look for excuses to do that, according to him, and we gave them one. So that's why he trashed the henhouse."

"'Trashed the henhouse,'" she repeated with sarcastic emphasis. "You make it sound like a jolly fraternity prank."

"Well, it was pretty extreme, sure. He's not a very stable individual, that goes without saying."

Yawning, stretching, he went to look through the back windows. She noted that he quickly averted his eyes and went to sit at the kitchen table.

Cracking eggs into the pan, she accidentally broke the first yolk, and then the second. With a muttered curse she hastily scrambled them all together.

"I find all this a little hard to accept," she said slowly.

"What?" He seemed genuinely puzzled.

"That someone should *violate* your home the way he did – kill Alice's dog – to say nothing of those lousy chickens – take a shot at you – at *us* –"

"Hey, wait a minute," he said, coming up behind her and squeezing her tense shoulders. "What are you so upset about? Don't you realize we almost had a war on our hands, and I stopped it? Are you trying to tell me that you're sorry I didn't shoot him?"

"Of course not!" she cried, twisting away from his hands. "But do you intend to leave it at this? Everything's just fine and dandy, now that you're pals with this sadistic halfwit, is that how it is?"

He returned to the table. Stiffly, he said, "It seems better than any alternative I can think of."

"I can think of a few." She dished the eggs out, annoyed with the leathery mess she'd made of them, then called, "Alice!"

"Like what?" he said, staring down at his dish in disbelief. She hoped he would say one word of complaint about the eggs, just one word, but he didn't.

"Like calling the police."

"They didn't do any good the first time. Even if we could convince the police to arrest him, what could they charge him with? Trespassing and malicious mischief, probably, and he'd be out on bail in a couple of hours and thinking up something worse to do to us. Be sensible, won't you? It's always better to get along with your neighbors, even if they are crazy, than. . . ."

He stopped as Alice came into the kitchen and kissed him on the forehead. Carol felt that her anger was in danger of boiling over and going out of all control, that she might soon be shrieking and hurling dishes. The fact that Dave was talking sensibly, and with such calm assurance, only made her angrier.

He wasn't reading her mood at all. It would have been better if he'd dropped the subject entirely, but he smiled wryly and said, "He said he'd do something to make up for the chickens. I got the feeling he plans to bag us an illegal deer."

"He must be crazy," Alice said. "How could you even talk to somebody like that, after what he did to Rags?"

Dave was disconcerted by this attack on his flank, Carol saw, even though he certainly should have expected it.

"Well, yes, he is crazy, but that dog I killed – it was more than just a dog to him, it was like one of his relatives. Even more. You could see it embarrassed him, but he started talking about the telepathic bond that existed between him and –"

"Another alternative would be to call Pete," Carol interrupted.

"Huh?"

"I said, another alternative would be to call Pete Jensen and tell him what his wife has got going with that bastard," Carol snapped. Too angry to consider her words, she added, "Maybe a real man would know how to take care of your new boyfriend."

"What the hell is that supposed to mean?" Dave demanded.

"It means that if Pete found out his wife was sleeping with Buster, he might give him the kind of beating he deserves, and –"

"No, no, no," Dave said, throwing his hands up, "Let's try to unscramble this whole mess you've just dumped on me. What do you mean, *boyfriend?* What's that supposed to mean?"

Now that she'd at last knocked a hole in his all-wise, all-knowing façade of fatherly competence, Carol had no intention of abandoning the attack. "I mean that you haven't been able to talk about anything else since you first saw this wonderful nature boy," she snarled. "I think there's something really sick about it."

"That's about the stupidest thing I ever heard you say," he said quietly.

"Then if it's so stupid, if it's so wrong, why don't you *do* something about that man? Why don't you call the police? Why don't you tell Pete that you saw his wife at Buster's house?"

"Because nothing needs to be *done,* for Christ's –"

In a low, fast voice that dripped concentrated venom, Alice leaned toward her and said, "What I think is sick, I think it's the idea of you threatening to call up some woman's husband and tell him she's having an affair with somebody."

"– sake," Dave concluded, looking bewildered.

"You stay out of this, miss!" Carol shouted. "I have no idea what you're talking about, but nobody asked you to butt into this discussion."

Alice shouted back, "I'll tell you just what I'm talking about, unless you stop yelling at Daddy for –"

"Stop it, both of you!" Dave said, and his chair crashed to the floor as he stood up. "I don't know what's gotten into everybody around here, but I think we all ought to forget it and try to start the day over again. I'm sorry I went running out of here like a maniac last night, and that's the only thing I'm sorry for. I guess it was upsetting to everybody, because that's just not the way I am, or the way I want to be. Well. I came to my senses, and I did what I thought was the right thing – what I know is the right thing. If you don't like what I did, then you ought to think about it for a while, because I acted out of my sincerest convictions – what I think are *our* convictions, all three of us."

"I didn't say –" Alice began.

"It doesn't matter what you said, the fact is, you were getting on your mother's nerves. Let's all try to cool off, huh?"

He righted his chair quietly and left the room. Carol expected Alice. to renew her assault as soon as he was out of earshot, and she tried to think of something to say to counter it. She couldn't. She had no idea how much her daughter knew, and anything at all that she said might be damaging.

She glanced up. Alice was scraping her and Dave's untouched dishes into the garbage. She put the plates in the sink and walked out without a backward look, letting the screen door slam behind her.

Carol sank back in her chair and let out a sigh. She hadn't touched her breakfast either, nor did she think she would. Her anger had faded, but it had left her stomach churning. She took a sip of coffee. It tasted good, even though it did nothing to improve the condition of her stomach.

She stared at the gun, lovingly oiled until its blue-black metal and brown wood held confusing, shimmery depths. It still dominated the room, just as it had dominated the argument. It was a symbol of this place. She couldn't even imagine it existing in their old apartment.

In New York, she had been Dave's equal. She wasn't his equal anymore, not here. He was exploring new areas of experience where she couldn't compete with him, in which she couldn't even begin to share. His unexpectedly masterful behavior during the power failure no longer seemed admirable. It marked the point where he had begun to cast her in a new role, the point from which he had led her into this nightmare.

Maybe it had been unfair to suggest a homosexual motive for his fascination with Buster Callan, but it hadn't been entirely unjustified. He and Buster had reacted to each other in a uniquely male way, a way that cut her out and left her a bewildered bystander. They had nearly killed each other, and then they had decided to have a good laugh over it. Without even knowing Buster, she could imagine him saying, "It's something a woman –" and he probably wouldn't say woman, he'd say *broad* or even *cunt* "– something a woman wouldn't understand." Dave, of course, would never say a thing like that. Not yet, anyway.

Jack would never put her down like that. Whatever faults he might have – and she found it hard to think of any at this moment – he didn't have a beer-guzzling, gun-toting, buddy-loving fantasy-self lurking inside his soul and waiting for the opportunity to take over.

Jack. How much did that little witch know? Nothing, of course. Alice had made a heated remark, a meaningless remark, and Carol's guilty conscience had provided emphasis where none had been intended. She'd said – what, exactly? – she'd said that it was sick to think of taking revenge through Pete Jensen. It would be wrong, she'd meant, for anybody to do such a thing. She hadn't meant that it would be especially wrong for Carol to do it. Of course. She didn't know anything about Jack.

She got up and dumped her own breakfast in the garbage. No more eggs; but now, perhaps, she could look forward to a month or so of eating venison, courtesy of Dave's marvelous new friend. Maybe he would start coming over for dinner, and he and Dave would drink beer and arm-wrestle and swap dirty jokes while she did the dishes.

She straightened up and stared at the telephone. The number of Pete's Tavern was stuck on the bulletin board beside it. All she had to do. . . .

Don't think, *do* it.

"Pete's Tavern, may I help you?" A woman's voice. The woman in question?

"Let me speak to Mr. Jensen, please."

"Ayuh, sure."

Odd echoes, obscure noises, then frighteningly, right in her ear, "This is Pete. Hello?"

"Pete?"

"Yeah, who's this?"

"I think you ought to know . . ." She looked away. By chance she found a sign, an omen to give her strength: a dooryard full of bloody chicken feathers. "I think you ought to know –" this was no time for euphemisms, but she had to swallow before the words would come out "Buster Callan is fucking your wife."

"Hey, what is this? Who are you?"

"They're absolutely shameless. They don't even bother to go indoors. The other day they were . . . *screwing,* right out in his front yard."

"What the hell!"

She hung up, congratulating herself on remembering to put in that detail about the *al fresco* fornication. Anybody could have passed by and seen that. He – and, more important, Buster – would never connect her with the phone call.

Chapter Fourteen

Buster had been going to Lettie Miller's general store all his life, but Lettie never failed to make him uneasy. Years ago, she'd caught him trying to swipe a comic book. He knew that she'd never forgotten it. She always kept a suspicious eye on him when he was in the store, waiting for him to try again – daring him, even. Her attitude enraged him, but there was nothing he could do about it unless he wanted to drive twenty miles out of his way every time he needed razor blades or shotgun shells.

"No, baby, you ain't welcome in here," he told Trooper, pushing the dog back into the car when he tried to scramble out. "One day maybe I'll bring you in here to tear the old witch's backbone out, but not today, unfortunately."

It occurred to him that this would be one of the advantages of being married: he could send Peggy to places where he felt uncomfortable or where he was downright unwelcome. He laughed out loud. Not even thinking about it, he'd pictured Peggy as his imaginary wife. He couldn't see any other woman as his wife.

He nodded curtly to the old loafers on the porch,

but they didn't intend to let him pass unscathed.

"Heard your dog got himself shot, Buster," one of the men said.

He turned to look at the man in the rocker. He was Frank Winter, a retired farmer who'd once had a run-in with his father over the sale of a pickup truck, and who had probably never forgotten it. Frank hadn't spoken two words to him in his entire life.

"That's right," Buster said, starting to enter the store.

"That's a shame, he was a smart dog," Frank said with patent insincerity. "You should've took better care of him, son."

Buster's grip on the screen door tightened. He felt a familiar chill in his extremities as the blood left them, preparing his body for violent action. He knew the signals. Unless he made an effort, he would lose control.

"Other dog's even smarter, Frank," he whispered. "You watch your goddamned mouth, or I'll show you his favorite trick."

His anger evaporated when he saw the pure terror in Frank's eyes. He was hot stuff, all right, scaring the hell out of old men in rocking chairs. He slammed the door after him as he walked heavily into the store.

"Don't you slam my door like that, Buster Callan, this ain't a barn, you know," Lettie Miller said in a shrill voice. "And stamping around on my floor like that with your dirty old boots is not going to make you seven feet tall, either."

"That old bastard ought to learn how to keep his mouth shut."

"You watch your language, too. You can just turn right around and walk outside again unless you can behave yourself. I don't need your nickel and dime business all that bad."

He was about to tell her what she could do with her store when her stern face softened uncharacteristically and she said, "I sure was sorry to hear about Ace, Buster. He was more like a human being than a dog."

He was stunned. Those were the only sympathetic words she'd ever spoken to him. She composed her face once more to its rigid angularity and added, "I hope you got no foolish ideas about getting even with the man who shot him."

Buster shook his head, laughing. "Don't ask me why, we're pals now."

It was obvious that she didn't believe him, but he would volunteer no explanation. He asked, "How come everybody knows about it?"

"I don't know, some fellows were talking at Pete's Tavern. You know how everything gets around as soon as it happens."

In other words, son-of-a-bitch Pete Jensen was crowing over his dead dog. He shoved the thought out of his mind and asked Lettie for a box of twelve-gauge shells. She looked at him with disapproval, as if she were going to remind him when the hunting season started, but she said nothing as she went to get his order.

He heard the screen door close behind him. He glanced back to see a woman who was worth a more thorough inspection. He turned and folded his arms, leaning back on the counter, and stared at her as she came forward. She ignored him.

"Hi," he said.

Her eyes flickered over him and instantly dismissed him. She was older than he'd thought at first – her slim figure, in tight jeans, was deceptively girlish – but he still thought she was worth looking at.

"You live around here, honey, or are you just passing through?"

This time she didn't even condescend to look at him. She was a classy, city-bred bitch, the sort of woman he'd never had. He supposed that having her would be easy enough, though, given the right opportunity. He wondered if the color of her dark-blond hair were genuine. He lowered his eyes to the snug vee of her jeans, trying to picture dark-blond hair there. The thought aroused him.

"What's the matter, don't you feel sociable?"

She turned her back on him and walked to the other end of the counter. She had a trimly rounded little ass, two firm handfuls. He followed her silently, and he got the satisfaction of seeing her jump when he spoke again, close to her ear.

"What say we go some place and fuck?"

"Get away from me, punk!" she snapped.

"Just trying to make conversation," he said easily, laughing. "I figured that was the subject that would interest you most."

"I told you to behave yourself," Lettie said, returning to the counter and banging down the shells. "Don't you mind Buster, missus, he's the closest thing we got to a village idiot."

He snorted with laughter as he pulled out his wallet. He paused, about to hand Lettie a ten-dollar bill, when he saw that the woman was now staring at him with open curiosity.

"If what you're doing is reconsidering my offer, it's still open," he said.

"Scat, Buster!" Lettie said. "Go away."

Surprisingly, the woman was blushing. It made her dark eyes bright. She averted them immediately.

"Last chance, sweetheart," he said as he pocketed his change. "You want me to wait outside?"

She faced him squarely and said in a cold, controlled voice, "Fuck off, you contemptible son-of-a-bitch."

Lettie gasped. Buster was no less shocked, although he tried hard not to show it. He laughed as he walked out. At the door he paused and said, "If you hadn't told me to watch my language, Lettie, I'd have an answer for this ten-dollar whore."

Frank Winter and the others had the sense to ignore him as he bounced down the stairs. He stopped short as he saw the station wagon beside his car. Even without the sign – PROTECT THE RIGHT TO ARM BEARS he would have recognized Dave Stern's car.

"Son-of-a-bitch," he muttered, and then he laughed.

He thumped Trooper affectionately as he got into his car. He started the engine, but he didn't leave right away. Maybe he ought to wait and apologize. Shit, he had nothing to apologize for! It had probably made her day to get a proposition from a man five or six years younger than she was. He banged his car into gear and left with a scream of rubber.

He had been feeling uneasy about making friends with the man who'd murdered Ace. Sparing him had been a sudden, inexplicable impulse. He did have to admit that the guy had balls for brains, chasing him a hundred miles an hour without headlights in those pussy pajamas. Beyond that they had nothing in common except intelligence. His ideas were just a lot of commie bullshit, and he would have been hopeless in the woods. He wanted to learn, though, as he had earnestly confessed after the fifth or sixth pitcher of beer. It seemed that Dave actually admired him and respected his way of life, and nobody had ever admired or respected him before.

But now he had a more convincing reason for cultivating Dave's friendship: getting into his wife's pants. He saw nothing wrong in that. If a guy couldn't hold on to his wife, that was his problem, not Buster's. She looked like the kind who would be hard to hold on to. She oozed sex with every motion. Even in her anger, even when she was trying to put him down, she had never seemed to lose her acute awareness of the fact that he was a man. Once she got started she would probably be ready for anything, too, a liberated city-bitch like that. She'd find it damned difficult to sneer at him and call him dirty names when she was kneeling on the floor in front of him with a mouthful of cock.

"What do you suppose Peggy's doing today, Troop?"

Trooper took that as an invitation to climb into the front seat, something Buster didn't normally allow. He decided to overlook it. He pummeled the shepherd's thick neck and fended off his playful nips.

"Fuck Peggy, I think we'll get us a deer for our old pal Dave. What do you say, Trooper, you want to kill a deer?"

The dog barked and, transported with enthusiasm, tried to climb into his lap. Buster managed to push him away with one hand as he steered. He tried to return the hand to the wheel, but Trooper held his wrist in his jaws with a gentle but very firm grip.

"Let go," he said, trying to pull his arm away.

The dog held on.

Buster looked at him. He didn't like what he saw in Trooper's yellowish eyes. It wasn't a killing look, but it was willful and malicious. The dog was testing him. His wrist looked small and frail in those jaws. He had spent long hours strengthening them, making Trooper hang by his teeth on a rope. Never mind a man's arm, those jaws could have broken a baseball bat.

"Let go, Trooper. Bad dog!"

He tugged. The grip firmed. A light growl rolled in Trooper's throat.

Buster was getting angry, but he forced himself to face front and ignore Trooper. Showing anger would be the worst thing he could do. In mastering a vicious dog like Trooper, you had to pick your showdowns carefully; and this was clearly no time for a showdown, with his arm in the dog's mouth.

Trooper growled again and gave his head a tentative shake, but he was still being careful not to break the skin or even use more force than necessary.

Buster laughed. He'd read somewhere that SS dog handlers used to file down the teeth of their attack-trained shepherds and Dobermans and replace them with steel caps. He'd toyed with the idea of having that done to Trooper, before he'd fully appreciated the dog's personality. The only thing that stopped him had been the expense.

"Sometimes I'm glad I'm poor, Trooper." He pulled the car onto a wide shoulder and cut the engine. "Okay, you want to play games with my arm, or do you want to kill a deer?"

Trooper let go, barked, and tried to do a dance in the tight confines of the front seat. Buster studied him for a moment. He had figured out why the dog was testing him. Now that Ace was gone, there was a vacancy in the family hierarchy.

He shook his head as he pulled a club from under the front seat and stuck it through his belt. He congratulated himself on his foresight. He had anticipated an argument over their next kill, and this time Ace wouldn't be around to protect him.

"You don't even know what this is, do you?" he said, patting the club. "Well, you'll find out if you don't mind your manners."

They went down through a bog where the deer sometimes browsed in the heat of the afternoons. They were out of luck, finding nothing but recent tracks. Buster resigned himself to the task of climbing to the high meadows. Trooper acted well until he caught a scent. Then he went wild, charging forward, barking, scattering every deer on the mountain.

Buster waited patiently on a mossy boulder until the dog returned, wagging his tail happily.

"The problem with you, you stupid cocksucker, is that you ain't a natural hunting dog," Buster explained. Trooper jumped up on the rock with him and licked his face. "Shit. You're all right when you got a partner who knows what he's doing, but you're hopeless by yourself. You just don't have the right instincts, you want to jump in headfirst and start killing." He brooded while Trooper waited, head cocked. If it hadn't been for his torn ear, he could have been posing for a calendar. "That would be just fine if I was running a concentration camp, but I'm not. You know; I should've taken up my new pal's offer to buy me a dog. You may not believe this, but the best dog on earth for hunting deer is a dachshund. Little bastards are smart, and they don't quit. That would be fine for the brains of this outfit, but I'd still need a big, mean motherfucker to keep you in line. A bullmastiff, maybe. Only he would still have to be one hell of a dog, big or not, or else you'd mop up the floor with him. Which is what you might wind up doing to me if I don't watch out." He ruffled the thick fur at Trooper's neck. "Oh, yeah, you're a handsome bastard, you think you're Rin Tin Tin the Wonder Dog. You're an asshole, that's what you are. You want to live in New York? I could sell you for a thousand bucks down there as a guard dog, and you could spend the rest of your life happily chewing on jungle bunny stickup men. I could buy a dachshund and a couple of Labs and still have enough left over for a night on the town."

Buster got up and stretched. A cold mist was coming over the mountain, and it could turn to rain in the next five minutes. He hurried down the trail. Now that he'd done all the damage he could, Trooper held his precise "heel" position.

"Only I've gotten attached to you, you son-of-a-bitch, that's the problem," he said as Trooper clambered into the car. "Well, when you're eating your Purina dog chow tonight, maybe it will occur to you why you're eating it. And maybe you'll try harder the next time."

It was raining by the time they got back to the house.

He hurried to the porch, hunching his shoulders against the rain, but he stopped short when Trooper began roaring at the front door.

"Oh, shit."

He gave the yard a hasty survey. No cop cars, thank God. He drew the club from his belt.

"Shut up, Troop. Who's in there? Speak up!"

He heard a soft groan. It was unmistakably a woman's voice. He went forward, letting the dog in first, struggling to adjust his eyes to the dark.

"Buster."

"Jesus Christ. What happened to you?"

He sank to the couch beside Peggy and took her in his arms. She winced and cried out at his touch. Her nose had been mashed out of shape. Its purple color blended with the puffy bulges of her tight-shut eyes. When she opened her swollen lips to speak, he saw a bloody gap where her upper front teeth had been.

The rain had made a lank mess of her Farrah Fawcett hairdo. Odd, but that seemed important to him as he catalogued her injuries.

"Who did this? Tell me. Peggy, he might just as well climb into his grave this minute. Who did it?"

She struggled with the name as if she couldn't bear to speak it. "P-Pete."

"Why?"

He saw that one of her ears was swollen, too. It was caked with dried blood.

"He found out. Somebody told him. Some woman called up and told him about us."

"Shit." Buster got up and paced, slamming his fist into his palm. "When did he do this?"

"This morning. He was acting funny yesterday, and then we went home and he started drinking and he kept asking me about you, over and over, and I told him, no, *no,* I told him, and I thought he believed me, and sometimes he'd cry and sometimes he'd scream at me, and I told him, *no.* He passed out on the floor and I went to bed, only I couldn't sleep all night. And then in the morning I dragged myself downstairs and he was awake, and he would only look at me, real cold like, and I was nervous and I couldn't help shaking and dropping things. And then he started to tick off all the times I had to go home sick, only they were really all the times we made love to each other, and he asked me, what did I have, three goddamned periods every month? And then I got mad and I shouted at him and told him how he was an old man who couldn't get it up anymore, and I told him how you were my boyfriend in high school and how I had your baby and everything, and I guess there wasn't much that I didn't tell him. And then he started hitting me. And he wouldn't stop, I couldn't make him stop, and when I fell down on the floor he kicked me, and I thought I was dying, only I woke up later and he was gone and I came here. Oh, Jesus, I hurt all over!"

"Yeah, this morning, that's okay, that's good. It will look all right. It's good. It'll look all right, if you can stay away from a doctor for a while longer, maybe twelve hours, nobody will know. Can you? Are any ribs broken, are you coughing up any blood?"

"Buster, what? What are you talking about? How do I know, is anything broken? I *hurt.*"

"Listen to me. Are you coughing up blood, or throwing up?"

"No no *no!*"

"Then it's probably all right. I'm sorry. I love you, Peggy."

She started to laugh, but then she cried out in pain. After she'd caught her breath, she said, "I guess you must really mean that, the way I must look and all. If you do, you won't kill him? What good is it to me if you spend the rest of your life in jail?"

"I'm not going to kill him. He's going to have an

accident, a horrible accident." He started to laugh. It was a high-pitched cackle, and its sound alarmed him so much that he cut it short. "Where's Bingo?"

"Buster, are you all right? I can't see your face. What are you talking about?"

"I'm talking about Pete's dog. Where's Bingo?"

"I don't know, Buster, he's at the house. What difference does it make?"

"Okay. Now, don't you go anywhere. You stay right where you are. Don't answer the door, whatever you do, don't let anybody know you're here."

"Don't do it, Buster, *please.* Stay with me, I need you. I love you, too, you don't know how much."

He sat beside her on the couch for a moment, afraid to touch her as she turned her blind eyes toward him.

"Who do you suppose told him?"

"He thinks it was that Mrs. Stern, the wife of the guy you wanted to shoot. He said she's the only one who talks snooty enough. I thought so, too. I answered the phone at the bar when she called him, and she's always calling there for her husband. Only this time she asked for Pete, and it was after that he started acting funny."

"It's a good thing I didn't shoot him. He would've missed all the fun." He stood up, then bent over, hesitating. He kissed her on the forehead. She reached out for him, but he evaded her hands. "First Ace, now you. My pal. I'll see you later. C'mon, Trooper."

Chapter Fifteen

As soon as the kitchen staff had cleaned up for the night, Pete herded the few remaining drinkers out the door. It didn't make much difference. Monday was always a lousy night for business. So was almost every other night.

When he'd locked the door after the last waitress, he phoned home again. This time he let it ring twenty times. Still no answer. That could just mean she was being stubborn.

It could also mean that she was lying dead on the kitchen floor.

He refused to accept that possibility. He'd hit her harder than he'd intended, he'd kept doing it longer than he should have, but she was a strong girl. When he'd left the house, she was still breathing.

He tried hard to suppress thoughts of Peggy as he totaled the day's receipts, but that was impossible. As soon as he managed to get his mind completely on his work, one or another of her blistering admissions would spring suddenly into his mind. Each time the pain seemed new. Familiarity didn't dull the edge.

In love with Buster Callan. Anybody else would have

found that funny. He tried hard, but he couldn't laugh at it. Traditionally, the whole situation was supposed to be a comic one. A man marries a girl twenty years his junior, and she then deceives him – it had been an old joke when Chaucer had used it.

He knew damned well she hadn't been a saint when he'd married her. He wouldn't have expected that or even wanted it. Whatever she did before he met her, that was none of his business. The only thing that mattered was that she loved him now, that she was his wife. This time he did manage to laugh, but he knew he didn't sound happy.

He poured himself a stiff shot of cognac and tossed it down, then poured another that he took to the cash register with him. All day he had resisted the urge to drink. He hadn't realized how much he'd needed it. He could feel muscles in his neck unknotting as the liquor took effect.

He went back to his work and was able to concentrate on it once more. Less than four hundred dollars. If he had many more days like this, he would be working for somebody else again. Business had been worse than usual this spring. As if things weren't bad enough, he had to meet the added expense of hiring a temporary waitress of the all-too-frequent days when Peggy didn't feel like working –

That time the memory came like a kick in the guts. He leaned against the bar, his mouth twisting as if to scream, but he made no sound. All those afternoons. With that rotten piece of slime. Cheating on him. Cheating him, too, cheating him out of money: the money he had to pay the temporary, and the tips that Peggy didn't get. He was more than generous with Peggy, he let her keep her tips; the other waitresses had to kick back half. And now that she wasn't making them, she was always badgering him for money. In effect, he was subsidizing her trysts.

And the bastard still had the nerve to come around here and sell him meat. Had the nerve to look him in the eye as he drank beer on the house, and all the time he was screwing Peggy. Well, Buster Callan wasn't the only man who jacked deer. He could do it himself, if it came to that, and he would save himself the expense of everything but a shotgun shell.

He hid the working cash for the next day in a concealed pigeonhole beside the sink, and stuffed the remainder into the bank bag with a deposit slip. He didn't plan to drive out of his way to the night depository, though. He would bank the money on his way to work in the morning. His main concern was getting home and seeing what the hell was going on.

He locked the door behind him. He had gotten out of the habit of giving the parking lot a thorough survey before stepping outside with the money. This was a lot different from tending bar in New York. He remembered his last job there, where the bank had been half a block from the bar. When he closed up at three or four in the morning, that half-block walk had seemed as long as any patrol he'd ever pulled in Korea.

As he slid behind the wheel of his car, he wondered if he should go back and get a bottle to bring home with him. He couldn't remember if there was anything left at home. Going back inside seemed like so much trouble that he realized for the first time how tired he was. He hadn't gotten any sleep last night.

Christ, she'd borne his child! And she was proud of that. They were meant for each other. The only drawback to their idyllic romance was that lover boy couldn't even support himself, much less a wife, but good old Pete would take care of that little difficulty. He would keep a roof over the slut's head for Buster's benefit. It was a wonder she hadn't whelped another of Buster's bastards and let Pete raise it, thinking it was his own. Maybe that would have been next on their agenda.

Don't think about that, he told himself. He snapped on the radio and found a Canadian station playing soft rock: Gordon Lightfoot, singing in French. It calmed him. Not knowing the language was a help; he didn't have to put up with words about true love or faithless love or any other kind of love.

For someone in a hurry to get home, he knew that he wasn't driving very fast. He still dreaded what he might find. What if he could have saved her life by getting her to a doctor this morning?

But she wasn't dead. She had probably run off. She had no relatives, at least none she got along with. Even though she'd grown up around here, she wasn't chummy with any old girl friends. So that left only one place she could go if she'd left home: Buster's. He laughed. He was sure that Buster wouldn't be overjoyed to have her turn up on his doorstep as a long-term guest. All that bullshit about loving only him and wanting to be with him forever – he would never buy that. She'd be back when she found out what living with Bigfoot was like.

He wondered if he should take her back. He felt inclined toward forgiving her. He could even understand her feelings, partly. He'd never been handsome to start with, and he'd let himself sag nut of shape. He was bald as an egg, most of his teeth came out at night, and his truss could hardly be considered an erotic stimulus. Peggy was young and full of energy. What energy he had left, he threw into his work. He liked to spend his spare time reading, and reading was a skill that she had never completely mastered. His only other hobby was hunting, and it had never even occurred to him to ask her if she would like to share that hobby with him. Maybe he would try that. They shared very little.

It was only natural that she should think longingly

of the high school boyfriend she might have married. Buster was eccentric and unpredictable and exciting; Pete was steady and reliable and dull. For the short haul, there was no contest. But he was convinced that she would eventually get sick of Buster, that she would come to her senses and realize where her own best interests lay.

Maybe he could even try to change himself for her sake, be more attentive to her needs and interests, take her to the places she would like to go. He had no idea what they might be. Parties, maybe, or dancing. The only place he ever took her was the movies, and only when it was a picture that he especially wanted to see.

He reined in his fantasies abruptly. She hadn't come back to beg his forgiveness. He didn't even know for a fact that she'd left him. She might be lying where he'd left her.

That goddamned uppity cunt and her wimp husband, they were to blame. What the fuck had Dave thought he was doing, going off to suck up to Buster Callan like that? Study the colorful peasants in their native environment? Gather material for a novel? Or just cause trouble? He had certainly accomplished the latter.

When Dave didn't return to tell him what had happened at Buster's, Pete became intensely curious. Nobody came looking for Dave, though, so it seemed safe to assume that Buster hadn't murdered him and disposed of his body. What must have happened was that Buster had beaten him up and Dave was too ashamed – or too seriously injured – to come in and talk about it. He had been tempted to call Dave up and ask him what had happened, but he had resisted the urge.

On Saturday night, he'd been busy for a change. During a break in the action, he surveyed the crowded room and spotted Buster Callan and Dave Stern at one of the tables. They both looked distraught and disheveled, like a couple of bums toward the end of a three-week drunk, but they were talking and laughing like old friends. It was doubly odd, since neither one of them was the type to make friends easily. Pete looked for them again when the business at the bar at last slowed down, but they'd left.

Then the phone call came from the wife. He didn't doubt her identity for a minute, and he almost called her back to let her know it. Her voice had a special, rusty squeak in it that he'd always found sexy, and she pronounced her words as if she had a mouthful of mashed potatoes. As if that wasn't enough, she had used her favorite word, "absolutely," and she had said it the way she always did, *absy.*

He couldn't figure it all out – although he hadn't tried very hard, not with the other thoughts that were burning trails of acid in his brain. Maybe Dave had arrived at Buster's house at the moment when, according to Mrs. Stern, he was screwing Peggy in the front yard. "Excuse me, sir," Dave had said, "but I'm afraid I shot your dog." And Buster, distracted by what Peggy was doing, had replied, "That's okay, think nothing of it."

That didn't sound plausible, but neither did anything else he could think of.

Whatever the circumstances, Dave had relayed the information about Buster and Peggy to his bitch of a wife. Why had she then made that call? Sheer malice, possibly. He'd known plenty of people capable of that. Or maybe she had wanted her voice to be recognized so that her husband would be made unwelcome at the bar. It seemed a drastic way of keeping your husband out of saloons. Maybe she was nuts. He'd never met her, and Dave had never said anything about her. He wouldn't talk about her, of course, if he had to keep her locked in the attic most of the time.

He was startled to find himself home. He had made

all of the proper turns without thinking about them. There were no lights showing in the house. In his headlights it looked abandoned and menacing. He kept the lights on and the engine running for a while. Bingo was yelping in his run. He probably hadn't been fed. He wouldn't have been, not if Peggy was still lying on the kitchen floor in the dark house.

He forced himself to go through the motions, to shut down the car and go to the front steps. Killing an unfaithful wife used to mean two or three years at most – he'd known a couple of men who'd done it. – but times had changed. He would probably draw a jury composed entirely of women's liberationists. The circumstances would count against him, too. He hadn't caught her in the act, and he'd killed her in a particularly brutal way. Maybe he could hide the body and just say that she'd run off.

Stop it, he told himself, she's right this minute lying flat on her back in Buster Callan's squalid hutch. Getting laid.

He pushed the unlocked door open.

"Peg?"

No answer. He turned on a light. The living room looked the same as it always did, with her astrology and confession magazines littered around the chair facing the television. He picked the magazines up out of habit and piled them on the coffee table.

"Hey. Peggy!"

He switched on the dining room lights. Nobody here but the ten-point buck over the fireplace, staring at him with glass eyes, the way Peggy would be staring at him when he got up the courage to push the swinging door and walk into the kitchen.

"Please let her not be dead," he muttered as he pushed through the door and snapped on the light.

He gazed for a long time at the spot where he'd left her, as if unconvinced that she was no longer there. He went to the kitchen cabinet and found that he hadn't drunk all the cognac. He poured an old-fashioned glass half full and sipped it before turning back to the sink, where he'd seen something out of the corner of his eye. Bloody towels. He picked them up, then dropped them. They told him nothing, except that she'd regained consciousness and tried to clean herself up.

Bingo was still raising hell in the backyard. That wasn't like him, hungry or not. Except when it came to hunting birds, he was a stolid, lazy dog. His barking sounded belligerent, the way it did when another male dog came around.

Pete went to the refrigerator for some ground venison. Buster had been right about that: nobody could tell the difference between venison and hamburger, and venison was a hell of a lot cheaper. He would have given Dave twenty bucks, maybe; for the carcass he'd buried, but it was a good thing he hadn't suggested it. A conscientious citizen like Dave would have run straight to the board of health, or else his wife would have, and to the game warden.

He mixed a fist-sized chunk of the meat with a larger helping of dog chow. He moistened it at the sink, ignoring the bloody towels.

Maybe she'd gone some place else to die – upstairs, maybe, or out in the backyard, and that's why Bingo was carrying on. What if she'd gone to Buster's place to die? He'd never get a chance to hide the body.

He suddenly brightened. If she had indeed died at Buster's, that was better luck than he deserved. The cops would never believe Buster's word against his, and he would swear that he'd never touched her, that he'd left her in the best of health this morning. That way, he would get both of them.

He would have to think about that, think hard. He would have to clean up, burn the towels.

He turned away from the sink; so preoccupied with

this new line of thought that he didn't, for a moment, realize just what he was looking at. When he did, it seemed that every muscle in his body jerked violently. Buster Callan and his dog were standing at the door to the dining room, watching him.

Shock gave way to rage. He took a step forward. The dog growled, but he paid it no attention. "What are you doing here?" he demanded. "What the hell do you want?"

"Trooper wants to show you his favorite trick," Buster said in a soft voice.

"Get out of my house, you scum, and take that mutt with you," Pete roared. "I ought to kill you."

"Yeah, I think you should have. I think that would have been a good idea. Only you should have done it before you went to work on Peggy."

Hearing this vile creature speak her name was more than Pete could bear. He wanted . to smash this arrogant little man; he wanted to demolish him utterly. His rifle was in the living room. His pistol was in the bedroom. He looked around for a weapon and spotted a cast-iron frying pan above the stove. He looked at Buster, who held the snarling dog's collar with one finger. God, that dog! Even without all the coarse fur, it would have weighed nearly two hundred pounds. It was bigger than its master.

Grab the pan, hit the dog with a backhand stroke – if he moved fast enough and hit hard enough, he would get a shot at Buster before he could react. In a brawl, Pete knew, the first blow was the deciding one.

But he couldn't keep his eyes off the dog. He felt some of his rage drain out of him, along with some of his courage. The back door was very close. Bingo wouldn't have a chance against this monster, but he might distract him and slow him down – if he could get out the back door and open Bingo's run quickly enough.

"What do you mean," Pete said, edging toward the door, "his favorite trick?"

It was hard to read Buster's expression in the shadow of his baseball cap, but now he smiled.

"Trooper," he said quietly, pulling his finger from the collar, *"hit!"*

"No!" Pete screamed, lunging for the door and struggling with the knob. It was locked. Buster must have locked it. "No!"

He was about to change his strategy and make a dash for the frying pan when a terrible weight hit him between the shoulders. His head was driven through the glass of the kitchen door. The vision in one eye was replaced by a clear white light of pain. He had to ignore it, because his right arm above the elbow was being crushed. It was being wrenched wildly from side to side as if it had been caught in a machine.

He struck clumsily at the dog with his left fist, but he only hurt his hand on its dense skull. He was jerked backward and flung down on the floor. The pain in his arm kept getting worse. He tore at the dog's fur without effect. He screamed, but he could still hear the slavering growls.

"Oh, Jesus God, my arm!" Pete shrieked. "He's got my arm off!"

"Sure looks that way," Buster said. "Hit, Trooper, *hit!"*

Pete lay on his back, kicking at the dog, but the dog ignored his kicks and went for his crotch. He tried to shield it with his left hand. But then he no longer had a left hand.

"You shouldn't've done that to Peggy," Buster said. "She's about the only friend I've ever had. Hit!"

Pete screamed, curling into a ball, trying to protect his face and neck with the spurting stumps of his arms. He remembered what Dave had said, that a creature attacked by a dog goes into shock and feels nothing.

Dave had been wrong.

"Hit!" Buster shouted.

Chapter Sixteen

Even after she had consolidated the contents of four tightly packed suitcases into three that were on the brink of explosion, Carol thought it still looked like too many for a short visit. But she had eliminated everything she could bear to leave behind. Leaving her favorite sweaters and winter coats had been the biggest struggle. But when she needed them, Dave would send them. It was impossible for her to imagine him being petty about such a request.

She had avoided telling anyone – even herself – just how long she planned to stay in New York, but she knew now that she wasn't coming back. She wouldn't tell Dave that, of course. She would be evasive when they spoke on the phone for the first week or two. After she was settled, after she'd found a job, she would write him a letter: She would tell him that she needed to be free to make it on her own for an unspecified length of time. She would tell him that the city was essential to her happiness, to her very life. She wouldn't state it bluntly, but he would know what she meant; a choice between their marriage and his insane experiment in country living. She wouldn't tell him about Jack. She might mention, in general terms, the need to ease the restrictive bonds of marriage.

She felt a desperate desire for a cigarette. Dave had gone out to buy them before noon. It was now past one. It was a ten-minute ride to the general store. Either he'd found a new saloon, or else he'd overcome his embarrassment about facing Pete. Damn it, she needed a cigarette! Getting one would mean walking six miles to the store and back, but she was almost ready to do it. Home in New York, at any hour of the day or night, she could have –

She spared herself the rest of that dreary litany as she heard the car pull up at the side of the house. She ran down from the bedroom and met him at the back door.

"You took your time," she said.

"Yeah, well." He fumbled in his pockets so ineffectively that, for a moment, she feared that he'd forgotten what he'd gone out for. One more second of that and she would have screamed – but he produced the pack. "Hell of a thing happened last night."

After inhaling deeply, she looked at him. She hadn't noticed, but he looked shaken.

"Pete Jensen beat up his wife."

"Because of Buster?" She coughed on the tobacco smoke. When she had recovered, she made her voice sound casual as she asked, "Did he find out about that?"

"Something like that, I guess, although Buster's name didn't come up in the gossip at the general store," he said. He must have been shaken. He had gone five minutes without realizing that he needed a drink. Now he corrected the oversight. He held up the bottle questioningly, and she nodded. "Nobody seemed to know she'd been carrying on with Buster. But it turns out she was the town tramp before she got married, and everybody was clucking about how they saw this coming. They took it as an opportunity to moralize about how the leopard can't change her spots. It was a little bit sickening. A lot of sanctimonious bullshit."

"How come they know all about this domestic dispute?" She sipped her drink. "Did she have him arrested?"

He laughed, and his laughter was singularly flat and humorless. "Arrested, yes, in the sense of 'stopped.' He's dead."

"Will you please for Christ's sake stop striving for melodramatic effects and tell me what happened?"

Her outburst jolted him. It jolted her, too. She made an effort to get herself under control.

"I'm sorry," he said, and he pressed her shoulder with his hand in passing as he went to sit at the table. "It's just that this is so – horrible, I don't know how to go about telling it. Maybe you're right. I'm so used to striving for effects in my stories that –"

"Dave, please," she said quietly, "what happened? Did she kill him?"

"No, his dog did. His faithful dog tore him to pieces. I mean that quite literally. This is really weird, because just last week he and I were talking at the bar, arguing about whether a man would go into shock if he were attacked by a dog –"

"Dave!"

"Oh, yeah." He finished his drink and got up for another. While he struggled with the ice cube tray, he said, "The way they heard it – and this is all third-hand, at best – he was beating her up. The dog was in the next room, with the door closed. She opened the door, and the dog flew right at Pete, protecting her. He did a very thorough job."

He returned to the table and sat opposite her. She turned her chair so she wouldn't have to face him directly. This wasn't her fault, she kept telling herself, but she was sure Dave wouldn't agree with her about that.

"Funny thing was, it was his dog, a hunting dog he normally kept in the back yard, not a house pet. And whoever heard of a killer Weimaraner? Bad – tempered ones, yes, but . . ."

She glanced at him. "You sound like you don't believe it."

He laughed again, this time with some humor. "'Mr. Holmes,'" he quoted, "'they were the footprints of a gigantic hound.' I don't know. Maybe I've been writing too many detective stories." He paused, then said, "You want me to drive you to the city tomorrow?"

"What?"

"Drive you to New York. I could stay over that night, make a few calls on editors in the morning, then be home by evening. It –"

She panicked. After all these weeks of anticipation, to be in New York and not be able to see Jack – it was unthinkable. "Oh, Dave, that drive is absolutely tiresome. I was looking forward to flying, really, and getting it over with."

"Well, all right," he said, seemingly only mildly disappointed. "It was just a thought. I've been meaning to talk to you about something serious, and on a drive like that, we'd have a lot of time for talking."

She stared at him. He knew. No, of course, he couldn't know. He was smiling.

"Why don't you tell me now?" she asked uneasily.

His smile broadened. "You were just complaining about my long-winded stories, and this promises to be the longest yet. It starts back in my childhood."

"We have until ten o'clock tomorrow morning," she said.

"Well, I'll tell you the ending first, although that's probably bad strategy." He looked down, frowning, and took a deep breath. She was alarmed. She didn't want to hear anything really serious from him, not now, and he seemed to be working himself up to a revelation of some importance.

"Maybe –"

"No," he interrupted, "no, I want to tell you. I'm fed up with myself. I'm disgusted with being what I am, a hack writer. No, no, that's what I am, don't say anything. I want to be a farmer. I mean, I want to make my living that way. And, in my spare time, use whatever talent I may have left to write something good, something I can be proud of – written the way I want to write it, without worrying about whether it will ever be sold or not."

"I always told you, you could write something good if you tried," she said, and she hesitated before adding, "but you never tried."

"I can't, not while I'm turning out garbage to support us. I don't get all that many ideas. When I do get one, I have to turn it into cash immediately; I can't save it for better things. Maybe that's inherent in this business, or maybe that's just how my own mind happens to work, but either way, it's an obstacle I can't overcome. I'd have to devote all my thinking, all my –" he made a deprecatory gesture "– creativity to the big novel. That's the only way I can ever get it written."

She stared at him. Good God, she was getting out in the nick of time. He planned to cut off his lifeline to civilization and to reality itself, and sink into the clutches of this soul-destroying place. She could see him in twenty years – if he lasted that long – a white-bearded eccentric, living on turnips and dandelion greens, with a trunkful of unsold novels in the attic.

"Dave, you said it yourself once – the only thing a writer needs is to be read. Shakespeare was a hack writer who had to make a living by appealing to the popular taste."

"I can see it now, the Shakespeare of the confession mags." He laughed bitterly. "That parallel just doesn't apply. Maybe that's my fault, but I know that I can't turn garbage into art, or even try to create art while I'm grinding out garbage with the other hand."

"But if you sit in a garret – or in a cabbage patch, that's more to the point – cultivating your own mannerisms for your own amusement –"

The phone rang.

"I'll get it," she said, rising. "Anyway, that was an argument you once gave me yourself, and I thought you were making sense then. Hello?"

"Mrs. Stern," said the woman's voice on the phone, "this is Peggy Jensen."

Her shock couldn't have been greater if the phone in her hand had changed into a rattlesnake.

"Can you hear me, Mrs. Stern?"

"Yes – yes, I'm here. I'm sorry about – about your husband."

Dave looked up, then rose from his chair. "What is it?"

"I don't owe you nothing, not after what you done to me," Peggy said, and Carol shuddered at the way her voice was slurred and thickened, "and maybe Buster will kill me for telling you this, but I got to tell you."

"I didn't do anything to you," Carol said. "I have absolutely no idea what you're talking about."

"I know what you did. I took that phone call; I recognized your rich-bitch voice. Don't bother to lie to me, that's not why I called. I called up to keep your kids from getting hurt."

"My kids? What are you saying?"

"What is it?" Dave demanded, but Carol impatiently waved him back.

"He says he's going to fix you that way; he says he'll meet your kids after school. He took Trooper with him."

"Who?»

"Trooper." After a pause, she said, "The dog that

killed my husband."

"Mrs. Jensen, wait a minute," Carol cried, but the phone had gone dead.

"What was that all about?" Dave asked as she replaced the receiver.

"That was . . . Dave, you'd better go pick up the kids at school. And take your gun."

He stared at her for a moment. "What are you talking about?"

"I'm talking about Buster. He's going to do something to the kids. That was Peggy. She said he's gone to the school – and he took Trooper, the Weimaraner."

Dave looked suddenly relieved. He sat back and lifted his drink again. "She's probably flying high on pain-killers, or else the beating did something to her head. Trooper is Buster's dog, a cross between a German shepherd and a dinosaur."

Carol could have screamed at him, but she forced herself to speak quietly. "She didn't say he was a Weimaraner. She said he was the dog who killed her husband.

"But it's still crazy! Why would Buster want to hurt the kids? We settled all that; we're friends."

She turned her back on him and stared out the window. He and Alice had cleaned up the yard. He hadn't replaced the chickens yet, but he said he was going to.

"I don't have time to argue with you, or explain, but Buster isn't your friend anymore. I called up Pete. I told him about his wife. She answered the phone, and somehow she recognized my voice. She blames me – and you, I guess. So does Buster."

She refused to turn around, even when the silence seemed to stretch on beyond all endurance.

At last he said softly, "You stupid cunt. You've really done it now, haven't you."

She whirled on him. "Goddamn it, go! It doesn't

matter what I did. I did what was right, what you didn't have the guts to do, I tried to fix that little bastard. Now why don't you go and do what you should have done in the first place? He's after your precious little filthy-minded witch of a daughter. Oh, God, what have I said, I don't even know what I'm saying, why don't you do something for a change?" She snatched up the rifle from its place by the door. "I'll come along and hold your hand, you don't have to be afraid of the nasty man and his bad doggie. I'll even blow his brains out for you, if you won't do it."

He got up and took the rifle from her.

"I think you ought to stay home and try to calm down, and maybe we can talk about all this later," he said as he went out the door. He hesitated, then turned back to her and said, "I don't expect any trouble. I'm sure I can handle this: I also think you should make a point of seeing a doctor when you're in the city. We'll talk about that."

"If you don't expect any trouble, why are you taking your stinking gun?" she shouted after him.

"I don't trust you alone with it," he said shortly.

She watched him go, but he didn't even glance in her direction as he climbed into the station wagon and drove off. Thank God she was leaving tomorrow. She couldn't have stood another day of this – or of him. He would probably go and get drunk with Buster again, and then they would be friends until the next time Buster went crazy.

Now that the initial shock had worn off and she'd had time to think about it, she felt no real fear for the children – not for the moment, anyway. Crazy or not, surely Buster didn't plan a kamikaze attack on a crowded high school with his savage dog. Perhaps he had intended to lure them somewhere; and the kids, with their New York upbringing, were not easily lured. But now Dave would be there. They could return home by well-traveled roads, and they would have the gun for insurance. Dave would never use it, unfortunately.

She worried about the future., though. Dave couldn't guard the children all the time. Buster might try again to strike back through them. She ought to take them with her. They weren't grown-up, regardless of what Jack said. But Alice wouldn't go; she wouldn't consider leaving her dear Daddy for a minute, and Mark – she didn't know what Mark would do. After she got settled, she could try to induce him to come down and stay with her, at least until the feud with Buster sorted itself out. It would do Mark good to associate with some intelligent people, to enjoy once more the intellectual stimulation that only the city could provide.

She returned to the bedroom for a final check of her preparations. Just the sight of the suitcase excited her. She was actually going! If only she were going now.

She felt tired and sweaty, as much from her emotional scene with Dave as from the job of packing. She needed a. shower. She decided it would be a good idea to wash her hair now, too, instead of waiting until morning. Stripped down to her panties, she studied herself for a while in the full-length mirror, trying to see herself with Jack's eyes. That was impossible. If you believed him, she was the most beautiful woman in the world. He believed it; he was, in the truest sense of the word, infatuated with her.

Surprisingly, she'd gained no weight since he'd last seen her. With no tennis, with no bags of groceries to carry four blocks from the market, she should have put on a few pounds. Maybe the reason was emotional strain, or maybe it was just because she couldn't get any of her favorite foods here in the wilderness. Whatever the reason, she was delighted. She knew that she was overly sensitive about the image she presented Jack, but one extra ounce would have made her feel like a dumpy old hausfrau.

Her breasts were small. That had been a mild trauma of her adolescence, but now she was glad of it. They were just as high and as well shaped as they'd been when she was eighteen, but they probably would have begun to sag by now if they'd conformed to the all-American ideal. Jack, of course, thought they were just perfect.

She stepped out of her panties and moved a little closer to the mirror. The stretch marks weren't terribly obvious, but she could see them. The knowledge that they were there always inhibited her from displaying herself as – as *wantonly* for him as she would have liked to. He loved to gaze at her body, to touch it, to kiss it, every last part of it.

"Oh, Christ," she groaned. "Control yourself, old woman!"

She fled from the mirror and tried to think of other things. It was difficult to think of anything but Jack. She could almost see him as he kissed his slow, teasing way up her thighs. She could almost feel him.

Halfway to the bathroom, she heard the car return. Dave hadn't been gone nearly long enough. Maybe he'd decided to play it safe by returning to call the school, or the police. Maybe he'd run into Buster on the way, and they had fallen into a tearful embrace and vowed eternal friendship once more.

She turned the shower on and adjusted the temperature of the water to her liking. About to step in, she paused. Maybe he would come upstairs. She felt a renewed quiver of warmth in her loins. He was angry with her, of course, but if she arranged to meet him in nothing but a seductively draped towel, he would probably get over it fast. After all, she wouldn't be seeing him for a long time, and . . . this might be the last time, ever. She smiled as she tucked the towel together, low on her hips, and went to the head of the stairs.

The children – well, he wouldn't have come back home unless that danger had been averted.

She heard an odd noise downstairs, like something metallic clicking against the bare floor. She had no idea what it could be.

"Dave!" she called.

She laughed as she recognized the noise. It was Rags, of course, the clatter of his claws.

Remembering, she screamed. At the same instant a huge, hairy thing bolted up the stairway. She covered her eyes with her hands and kept screaming.

"Hold!" a man bellowed. She heard boots thudding on the stairs. In a conversational tone, he said, "What that command means, it means he will take you apart if you blink an eyelash."

"No," she sobbed, "go away, get out of here."

She looked again. The dog was no more than three feet away, watching her with an ominously alert expression in its yellow eyes. She dropped her hands to cover her breasts. The dog showed its fangs – its tusks. The towel came undone and fell to the floor. Instinctively, she snatched at it, but the dog roared at her. She stood naked and shivering, afraid to move a muscle, as the man squeezed past the dog.

"Please," she said. "Please go away."

"Sure," Buster laughed. "But not for a little while yet."

She shuddered as his hard hands began to stroke and explore her body. She squeezed her eyes shut.

"I thought you would both run off to protect your kiddies," he said, "so I come over to burn your house down. Fucking you will be better, though. Less destructive, anyway."

"Please."

"You don't need to say please. I'll give you all you want."

He pushed her toward the bedroom, not roughly. He wasn't at all rough or brutal. It amazed her, because she had never felt hands like his on her body. They were like tough leather, but he used them gently as he guided her down onto the bed.

It was as if she had been in a trance and were only now waking. What was happening to her? She pushed him and tried to disengage herself from his embrace. "No, I don't want you to, no, please, don't," she muttered.

She couldn't seem to push hard enough. He overcame her efforts easily; she didn't even slow down his progress as he undressed. She was aware of the dog watching them, but she didn't dare look at it. She looked at Buster's face hovering over her. It wasn't, in itself, a frightening face; it could even be called good-looking, but its unfamiliarity was frightening. It didn't belong here, it was wrong, he shouldn't be . . . entering her like this.

"I'd hate to see you when you do want it," he chuckled, shifting his position to thrust deeper. "I think you'd scare me."

"Be quiet!" she said. "Just don't say anything, all right?"

Her body had betrayed her, and now she no longer even tried to suppress its urgent needs. She wound her legs around him, digging her heels into the small of his back, and met his thrusting eagerly. She rolled her hips, syncopating his rhythm.

Her feeling shifted when he clamped his lips down on hers. She was able to participate with him in a purely animal function, but any hint of human tenderness disturbed her. It reminded her how much she despised him.

The letdown was only temporary. It flickered past, and her excitement returned with awesome force. She moaned and whimpered as she struggled to break through the cage of her body and fly, and then suddenly she was free and flying, kissing him again and again as he grunted and began to thrust less surely.

"Buster?" she said, after they had both come.

"Mm?" His face was buried in her shoulder.

"Would you do something for me – promise me something?"

"Probably not," he sighed, pushing himself up and withdrawing. "What I ought to do is take you over to have a look at Peggy, and then I should give you about one-tenth of what Pete gave her, which would be the worst pain you ever felt in your goddamned useless life."

He sat up and began pulling up his clothes. The dog watched them from beside the bed, its long tongue hanging out.

"Did that dog really kill Pete?"

He stared at her. She suddenly remembered that she was naked and snatched a corner of the bedspread to cover herself.

"Who told you that?"

"Peggy did."

He looked away and resumed pulling on his boots. "She doesn't know what she's talking about. His own dog did it."

"What I wanted to ask you – don't hurt my kids. You won't, will you?"

He patted her hip. The gesture was one of affection and proprietorship, and she tried to conceal her involuntary shudder of disgust at the familiarity.

"I wouldn't've hurt them in the first place," he said. "That was just what you call a diversion." He looked at her. "I won't hurt them, don't worry, nor your husband."

"Thank you."

"I'll be back to see you, though," he said, rising and walking to the door.

But, thank God, she wouldn't be around. She closed her eyes and listened to his receding footsteps and the click of the dog's claws on the stairs. The shower was still running. She slid out of bed and went to it.

There would be no point in telling Dave about this. She didn't want anything to interfere with her trip.

Chapter Seventeen

Trooper was being a model dog today, but maybe that was because there were no deer around. Buster had been out for three hours, and he hadn't found any recent signs in the likeliest places.

"Ought to give you a fat-assed bartender to chew on every day. It seems to do wonders for your disposition," he said, and Trooper wagged his tail.

He knew that he was whistling in the dark. He'd spoken to the dog that way to quiet his own growing uneasiness. Trooper's personality had undergone a subtle change since he'd sicked him on Pete. He had never been afraid of humans; but now that he'd seen for himself what creampuffs they were, it was obvious that he held them in contempt.

The secret of training an attack dog, as Buster saw it, was to find a pup with a strong ego and work to make it even stronger. But after Trooper killed Pete, his ego ballooned out of all proportion. He now waited a couple of beats before obeying any command. Sometimes he flatly refused to obey, and then he would try to engage in a staring contest with his master.

Worst of all, Buster's feel for Trooper – never very

strong with this dog – was gone. There was no mental contact, no sense of identity with the animal. He had no idea what Trooper might do from one minute to the next. His club was stuck through his belt now, and his hand was never very far from it.

As if he didn't have enough troubles, the police weren't buying Peggy's story. They hadn't come right out and told her that yet, but he was sure they would. He'd thought that he was being remarkably clever, a regular criminal mastermind, arranging Pete's death the way he had. Only when it was too late had he seen all the dumb mistakes he'd made.

First of all, Bingo had been impounded. Peggy – on his advice – had urged the police to destroy him, but they said he was "evidence." Anticipating that, Buster had taken the precaution of smearing Bingo's coat with Pete's blood. That part of the evidence was fine. But the police had certainly taken pictures of the scene, and some bright boy might notice that the bloody prints all over the kitchen floor had been made by paws twice the size of Bingo's.

That little detail hadn't occurred to Buster at the time. If they went that far, they might take impressions of Bingo's teeth and compare them with Pete's wounds, which would be like comparing a nip from a crab with a bite from a shark.

His worst mistake, of course, had been running over to hold the Widow Jensen's hand on the day after the murder. His visit had been noticed. The cops hadn't questioned him yet, but he didn't doubt that they would. He had told Peggy that they had to stay away from each other for a while. She hadn't liked that, and neither had he.

He still had a second line of defense. Even if the cops decided that Trooper had killed Pete, Buster could tell them a plausible story. He was a friend of the family, an old schoolmate of Peggy's. When Pete beat her up, she came to him for help. He went over to talk to Pete and see if he could straighten things out. He took his dog with him because, as everybody knew, he took his dog with him everywhere. Pete wouldn't listen to reason. He accused him of butting in, and then attacked him. The dog, trained to protect Buster, did his job.

There were holes in that story, sure, but an expensive lawyer could plug them. Peggy had money now. If she let him down, he could put his farm on the block.

The cops would bounce him off the walls a lot, but he could take that. What infuriated him was the prospect of some sadistic asshole putting a bullet through Trooper's head to save the world from a killer dog. He thumped Trooper's side, and the dog responded by clunking those bear-trap jaws a fraction of an inch from his hand; but he knew that was intended affectionately.

The third line of defense, if it ever got that far, was a mess. A hyperactive prosecutor might try to make a case against him and Peggy of conspiracy to commit murder and cover it up. His star witnesses would be the Sterns. Dave could testify that Peggy and Buster were lovers before the murder. His wife could testify that she had tipped off Pete, just before his death. And, thanks to the moron he had the misfortune to be in love with, she could also testify that Peggy had threatened her with "the dog who killed Pete."

He stopped short, shaking with rage. When he'd heard that one, he'd almost lost control. He'd told her exactly what to say over the phone, he'd rehearsed her in it, but she'd gotten the inspiration to add that juicy little detail.

Trooper had stopped, too, and was looking at him questioningly. "Listen, baby, you got it good," he said. "Your bitches can't talk."

He started walking again, up toward one of the ski runs. He couldn't sell deer meat to Pete anymore, unfortunately, but he and Trooper still had to eat.

His mood brightened slightly. Carol Stern hadn't told anybody he'd raped her, if you could call it that. At least her husband hadn't come gunning for him. According to Lettie Miller, Carol had caught a bus at the store this morning, chattering about how she was going to fly to New York and how happy she'd be to spend a few weeks down there. Maybe he ought to go down there and look her up. When she proved to be such a pushover, his first reaction had been one of annoyance. He hadn't intended to screw her for her amusement. He had to admit, though, that she was damned good at it.

"Should've left those goddamned people alone," he muttered to his dog. "Or they should've left me alone. They got no business up here in the first place."

Trooper lunged ahead, barking. Buster grabbed his choke collar, and for one fearful instant it seemed that the dog was going to drag him off his feet or dislocate his shoulder. He braced his legs and hauled, lifting the dog's forequarters and half strangling him. He got a closer grip when Trooper turned, fangs bared, and tried to get at his wrist.

"No, you bastard, no!" he roared, drawing the club.

Unable to breathe, Trooper decided this wasn't worth all the trouble. Buster eased his grip slightly.

"Good boy," he said. "Calm down, that's the boy, take it easy. I hope to Christ that wasn't a deer you were barking at."

He kept a light grip on the shepherd's collar as he came up to the edge of the run and walked out into the open. A big kid stood there, looking guilty.

"What are you doing?" Buster asked.

"What's it to you?" The boy had been stuffing something into his pocket, and now he took his hand out and folded his arms too casually. Trooper didn't like him. He was all but foaming at the mouth, and Buster tried to conceal the trouble he was having holding on to him.

"Listen, kid, he thinks you're dog food, and I might let him go. What are you doing?"

"Planting stuff. You're Buster Callan, aren't you?"

"Ayuh. *Sit,* you bastard!"

"What you need is a whip and a chair with that thing," the kid said.

Buster didn't like the way he said "cheh," but the kid didn't seem to be laughing at him. Trooper finally sat.

"Did you follow me up here to get me?" the kid asked.

"Huh? I don't know what you're talking about."

"My Dad said somebody told him you were going to kill me. I'm Mark Stern."

"Oh, Christ. Some stupid cunt said that, I didn't. Her old man rattled her brains around for her, so she started hearing voices."

Mark sat on his heels. Trooper watched his every move with intense interest, but Buster felt he could let go of the collar. Trooper continued to sit.

"I figured it was some kind of misunderstanding. Like when Dad shot your other dog. He didn't mean to do that, you know."

"So he told me. The dog's still dead, though. What were you planting?"

Mark reached into his pocket. Trooper tensed in every muscle at the sudden movement, and Buster laid a hand on his shoulders. He sat down opposite Mark, cross-legged, his arm draped loosely around the dog.

"Don't make any sudden moves, not with this prick," Buster said. "He thinks he's hell on wheels lately."

"I thought you could talk to dogs," Mark said, "and that you often got answers."

"Not him. What, was your father, talking about me?"

"No, the kids at school." Mark extended his hand slowly with the plastic bag in it. Buster took it. "To hear them talk, you're a combination of Davy Crockett and the Wolf Man."

"They never did like me much at school."

"That isn't what I meant," Mark said, while Buster wondered why he'd made such an admission. "They think you're great."

"Bullshit."

"No, I mean it. Everybody's got a Buster Callan story. Like how they saw you beat somebody up, or how they saw you make your dog do some real complicated thing, as if you'd transferred minds with him. When I heard that you were a friend of my father's, I was proud of him. I never expected it, you know. I mean, I never thought all that much of him."

"He's not a bad guy," Buster said, examining the bag. It contained round, greenish-brown seeds. "I heard your mother took off for New York City this morning."

"Yeah. I would've liked to go with her, but . . ." He shrugged. "She never listens to anything I say."

Buster was embarrassed. The kid couldn't keep his mouth shut; he seemed bent on telling him the story of his life. How do you talk to a kid when you've just raped his mother? He held up the bag. "What's this stuff?"

"Pot."

"Oh. Some guys in the Army used to smoke it, and then they would act stupid for a couple of hours. I never did."

"They never asked you, huh?"

Buster looked at him sharply. He saw no suggestion of mockery. "That's about it," he said.

"I figured I'd plant some up here," Mark said, gesturing at the ski run near them. He saw that Trooper was still following his every move, and he slowly extended his hand toward the dog. "C'mere, pooch."

Buster disengaged his arm. Trooper stood up and stretched his muzzle toward the hand, sniffing. Mark held his hand still, making no move to pet him.

"That's how you do it," Buster said. "Let him get to know you."

"You want to smoke?" Mark asked.

"I don't smoke. Never did."

Mark laughed. Trooper was letting him chuck him under the chin now. Buster was impressed.

"I mean, a joint. It's funny, you know, here you are, a local legend. And sitting here with you, I expect at any minute that springs and wires are going to come popping out of your head. You have to mellow out, you know?"

Buster studied him hard, but the kid still didn't seem to be laughing at him.

Having satisfied his curiosity about Mark, Trooper went off on a romp, chasing a cluster of little white butterflies across the ski slope. Mark pulled a green cigarette from the pocket of his shirt. He lit it, drew deeply, and passed it to Buster.

Buster took the cigarette, but he hesitated. "Listen, I can't afford to get stupid. I have to watch that son-of-a-bitch every minute."

"This will expand your mind," Mark said in a strained voice, not breathing. At last he exhaled the smoke and said, "You'll be able to talk to him better."

"That would be helpful," Buster said, drawing the smoke deep and instantly coughing it up: "Shit!"

"Slow and steady. Just take it down with some air, then hold it for a while." He took the joint and demonstrated.

"It's ironic, you know," Mark said, passing the joint. "I think the country sucks. So does my Mom. She's been climbing the walls for weeks; she couldn't wait to go back home."

"It wasn't a spur of the moment thing, huh?" Buster asked, trying to sound casual' about it.

"Oh, hell no, she's been planning it. Like I said, I wanted her to wait till school was out so I could go with her. Anyway, that's beside the point, which is that my Dad is the one who loves the country. He has this thing about wanting to live off the land. And yet I'm the one who's doing it. I made a couple of bucks last year off the stuff I grew."

"You mean, you're a dope pusher?"

Mark laughed and fell back on the grass. "Come on, man! Give me a break. What've you got, this idea of me going around to playgrounds and turning little kids on? Everybody smokes; it's like a social thing. The way drinking used to be."

Buster was, having more success with the joint now. He found that he could hold the smoke down. He passed it back as Mark sat up. He watched Trooper galloping toward them. The dog's progress was oddly discontinuous. It was as if Buster was looking at a series of still, snapshots of the dog, each one larger than the last.

"I can't say it does anything for me," he said.

"It's subtle," Mark said. "You have to accustom yourself to the effect. It doesn't club you over the head, the way booze does."

Trooper ran over Buster, knocking him flat on his back, and kept on going. He lay staring at the sky for a while. He took the cigarette that Mark handed him and inhaled.

"He thinks he's God," Buster said. "That fucking dog. I've had dogs – I won't tell you about some of the dogs I've had; I'll just say that I've known a lot of dogs very well."

"Dogs, yeah, I can dig that."

"I've had dogs. Do you follow me?" Buster said, dazzled by the complexity of the thought he was struggling with.

"Ayuh," Mark said.

"Dogs. What was I saying? Anyway, some of them – Ace, for instance, he thought he was a human being. I don't know how he justified it, he must have known he had four legs and a tail and all, but he thought he was a person. He honestly believed he was a human being."

Buster sat up and looked at Mark, who was much farther away than he had remembered. It seemed as if he were looking at him through the wrong end of a telescope.

"And I thought he was a human being, too, that's the point. That was the dog your father shot."

"Easy, easy."

"No, I want to tell you. That dog ways like a lid on Trooper, and now that he's not here, Trooper just keeps getting bigger and bigger ideas. It used to be that I would think something and Trooper would do it. Now it's like he thinks up things, and I have to do them."

"Heavy," Mark said, passing the joint.

Buster inhaled. He felt Trooper's teeth press lightly on his neck. He heard a low purr of a growl and smelled the dog's fetid breath.

"You see this?" Buster said. "I don't dare move now. You were saying how I talk to dogs. Well, this one talks to me. I think he must have heard what I was telling you, and now he's telling me that he's going to break my neck if I don't keep in my place. Son-of-a-bitch thinks he's God. He tells me what to do. It was him who wanted to go and kill Pete, not me."

Buster sat thinking for a moment. He had the impression that he'd said something wrong, but he couldn't remember what. It was hard to hold on to thoughts from one minute to the next.

"I made a mistake," Buster said. "I don't like this stuff at all. Now I know why they call it dope."

"You'll get used to it. Does he know any tricks?"

"Tricks? Shit, yes, look at this trick. He's been holding onto my fucking neck for the past three hours. I'm getting goddamned sick of it, Trooper. Christ. This is embarrassing."

"He loves you," Mark said. "He's just playing. Right, Trooper?"

Trooper's growl sounded to Buster like distant thunder.

"Let go of my neck, Trooper, I'm not kidding."

"Does he chase sticks?"

"Chase sticks? Jesus Christ, the fucking dog has got me in a death-grip –"

"You're exaggerating," Mark said, standing up. "You're still too uptight, you should smoke some more. Hey, Trooper! Come on, boy!"

Trooper's growl deepened. Saliva trickled down Buster's spine.

"You better sit still," Buster said. "You're distracting him."

Mark picked up a stick and raised it to his shoulder. The grip left Buster's neck instantly. When Trooper sprang, he seemed to leave a gold smear in the air behind him that marked the course of his flight. For a moment Buster was transfixed as he studied this phenomenon.

Then he heard the screams, and he saw the red splashes that Trooper was flinging from side to side as he wrenched his big head this way and that.

"Trooper, no! No!"

He struggled with the choke collar and flung his full weight down on the dog. He managed to tear him away from Mark Stern's throat, but not before it was far too late.

Chapter Eighteen

". . . And we have something you don't have," Carol said. "A weir. Do you know what a weir is, Jack?"

Jack knit his brows together lovably. "I think it's something like a tarn," he said at last. "It's one of those Scrabble words I've looked up maybe twice in my life and forgotten the meaning of."

"I thought you were supposed to be an English teacher," she teased.

"English is what people speak, not –"

"Bullshit," McTeague said. He was a shaggy poet with a luxuriant red beard who had surprisingly replaced Brad Cohen as Cissy Parker's "roomie" during Carol's absence. She was impressed that he could wear a coarse wool sweater with nothing under it, as the many moth holes testified. "Most of the girls I knew at Berkeley had a vocabulary of three words, 'wow,' 'man,' and 'fuck,' in all their permutations of meaning – and the English language is somewhat richer than that. A weir is a small dam."

"He knows everything," Cissy said, not for the first time, shaking her head slowly in admiration.

"I also know why our friend the English teacher –"

he made those words sound like a mortal slur "– associates a weir with a tarn. He's thinking of Poe's lines –

"It was hard by the dark tarn of Auber,
"In the misty mid-region of Weir.

"Incidentally, Poe was trying to be evocative by taking the name Auber from a lousy composer and the name Weir from a lousy painter of the Hudson River School, because he thought their work fit the mood of his poem."

"Poe sucks," Jack said, and Carol squeezed his knee.

"I couldn't agree with you more," McTeague said, raising his glass in a toast toward Jack.

"But you've left your weir for good, is that the idea?" Cissy asked. Carol had forgotten that Cissy, an elegant blond now wearing an equally elegant lounge suit of black silk, could often make her feel dowdy.

She was spared an immediate answer by McTeague, who said, *"Farewell to the Weir.* Think of the gushy novel that could be written around such a title."

Carol sighed. She felt far more at home in Cissy's apartment, with its high ceilings and toylike fireplaces, than she had ever felt in that farmhouse. The tame jungle of plants in the window was infinitely preferable to the forests of the Green Mountains.

"I'm pretty sure, yes. I'm going to try to make it on my own for a while."

"Not entirely," Jack said.

She looked at him with a smile. "Yes, there's going to be a big place in my life for you. But for a change, it's going to be *my* life, so don't expect me to cook you breakfast or wash your socks, Jack." She turned back to Cissy. "The first problem is a job. I've been a housewife for – my God, eighteen years. I wouldn't even know where to start looking."

"Here's to divorce," McTeague said. "If it weren't for that institution, where would we get all our cocktail waitresses?"

Jack laughed, but he cut it short when he saw that she and Cissy weren't amused. The remark had cut far too close to the bone for Carol's liking.

"I need a drink," McTeague said, getting up. "Anybody else?" No one looked at him, and he carried his glass off to the kitchen.

"He's wonderful," Cissy sighed, "but he drinks like a fish. And he manages to insult everybody sooner or later."

"I don't feel insulted," Carol said. "He stated my problem bluntly, that's all. Do you have any ideas about it, Cissy? It looks like it's either waitress or topless go-go girl – only I'm too old for that."

"No, you aren't," Jack said quickly. "I've known eighteen-year-olds – who weren't – I mean –"

She patted his cheek. laughing.

"What did you do before you got married?" Cissy asked.

"I was in college; majoring in art history – and by the way, Jack darling, I never heard of a painter named Weir, either."

"Don't worry about a job," he said. "You can stay with me as long as you like. Forever."

"Don't crowd me, lover," she said, kissing him lightly on thc lips. "I'd like to get into publishing – some art book house, maybe. Doing exactly what, I don't know, but I'm sure I could make myself useful. You don't have any contacts there, do you, Cissy?"

"Contacts," McTeague grumbled, returning with a large glass full of gin. "Contacts. That's the magic word, here in the Emerald City."

"I'll ask around," Cissy said, ignoring him. "The thing to do is to go around to all those places, try to talk to someone and watch the ads in the *Times.* I hope

I'm not being tactless, but what does Dave think about all this?"

Carol looked down at her glass. "He thinks I'm spending a week in the city."

"William Blake never had to worry about contacts," McTeague muttered, "except with God, possibly."

"If you don't mind my saying so, you should have told him your plans. You're only making a bad scene worse by postponing it," Cissy said. "And he's not such a bad guy. He might even have helped you with some contacts in the publishing business."

"That place, Cissy – you can't even begin to understand. It sapped all my strength, all my will. The house, the land – it was like a vampire. I couldn't talk there, I couldn't even think. There was a man – what do you call those evil creatures who live in the deep woods and lurk under bridges and things?"

"Trolls," McTeague said.

"Thanks. He was a troll. He attached himself to us; he became a kind of obsession with Dave. Dave happened to kill his dog by accident, so he came back and hung our dog from a tree."

"Not Rags!" Cissy cried.

Carol nodded. "Then he killed all our chickens."

McTeague tried hard to contain his laughter, but it sputtered out.

"No, don't be mad at him, Cissy, really. I know how funny it must sound down here in the real world, among real people. You can't understand what it was like to be besieged like that. He had a horrible dog who was like every childhood nightmare about the Big Bad Wolf. He used it to kill a man. And then he . . ."

"Hey, what's the matter?" Cissy asked, leaning forward to clasp her knee. "Are you all right?"

"She needs another drink," McTeague said, getting up and taking her glass. "Fortunately, she has the right contact for that."

It was easier to say it, all in one breath, when McTeague had left the room, "And then he threatened me with the dog and raped me."

"My God!" Jack said. "You're kidding."

She managed a smile. "That isn't the kind of thing a woman jokes about, Jack."

"What did you do?" Cissy asked.

"Nothing. What could I do? I wanted to get away. I didn't want to explain how I'd been raped to a bunch of hayseed cops and then spend months hanging around to testify. All I wanted to do was leave."

McTeague returned with a. fresh drink and handed it to her. She thanked him, and he asked her, "Did you come?"

She stared at him, slack jawed, unable to believe that she'd heard correctly.

Jack sprang to his feet. He experimented with a variety of facial expressions. He seemed incapable of speech. His fists were clenched. She reached out to grasp his forearm. He seemed willing to be restrained. He sank to the couch as McTeague turned his back and strolled away.

"That's the classic question asked by policemen, according to women's groups," McTeague said.

"I think you're completely out of order," Cissy said icily. "This is too much, even for you."

"No, no, not at all. I'm curious. About the police, partly, why they should ask such a question. Does an orgasm make the crime seem less reprehensible to them? Are they concerned, for their own private reasons, with determining whether the complainant is *a hot piece?* Do they, for legitimate investigative reasons, want to find out whether the rapist is good at what he does?"

"You're an asshole," Jack said.

"And you, sir, are a teacher," McTeague said, turning to face them when he had reached the windows. "And

I'm partly concerned with Carol's answer to my question. When she told us about the massacre of the dogs and the chickens and the cats and the hamsters and the goldfish, her expression was suitably grief-stricken. But when she told us of the rape – and here, Carol, you must forgive me for lurking at the kitchen door, but I sensed that you were on the verge of a momentous declaration – when you told us of the rape, a most inappropriate smile appeared on your lovely face. I put it to you, Mrs. Stern, that you were not an entirely uncooperative victim –" here he adopted the pose of a British barrister, clutching the front of his moth-eaten sweater as if it were a judicial robe "– and I must ask you once again: did you come?"

Carol looked him straight in the eyes, which were bloodshot and ever so slightly unfocused., "As a matter of fact, yes, I did."

"Christ," Jack said.

She turned and stared at him. He was unwilling to look at her as he said, "This conversation – I think it's in extremely bad taste. This is all very painful for me."

McTeague roared with laughter as he returned to his chair beside Cissy.

"And I don't think the crime is any less reprehensible for that," she said, again facing her cynical tormentor.

"Nor do I," McTeague said. "I find drinking extremely pleasurable –"

"You can say that again," Cissy muttered.

"– but if someone were to force me at gunpoint – or, if you wish, at dogpoint – to drink, I would deeply resent it. I would consider it a violation of my privacy, my free will."

Carol felt a pang of indefinable emotion as she realized how much Dave would have enjoyed sparring verbally with McTeague. Mark's reaction would have been very much like Jack's: he would have glowered sullenly at this drunken buffoon. The thought shook her. Was she attracted to Jack because she saw something of her son in him?

"But," McTeague went on, "if I were nonetheless able to enjoy my indulgence in alcohol, even under coercive circumstances, then I would congratulate myself on my sensuality. As you, dear lady, should congratulate yourself on yours, without retreating one inch from your just condemnation of the felon." He raised his glass. "Confusion to all dogs and rapists!"

"I'll drink to that," Carol giggled.

"Isn't he marvelous?" Cissy said, gazing at her new roomie. "I never thought he'd be able to talk his way out of that mess."

"I think we'd better be going," Jack said.

But they didn't go, not immediately. Carol still had innumerable questions to ask about friends they shared, places they knew. McTeague had a multitude of toasts to propose the restoration of the Stuarts, the return of the Latin Mass, human reproduction by cloning, the poetry of Andrew Quarles. Jack tried to talk to McTeague about Piaget, but McTeague summarily dismissed him as "that pinko frog." It was only when McTeague had tottered off to the bedroom and collapsed noisily on the floor that they took their leave.

Carol tried to prevent Jack from squandering money on a cab from 110th Street to the Village, but he insisted. As their taxi crawled through the bright, steamy enticements of Times Square, he said, "When I was a kid in Asbury Park, New Jersey, my idea of – of what would you call it? Class? Success? All that, yes, and the ultimate good time – it was riding through New York City in a taxi with a beautiful woman. And now I'm doing it. You've made my dream come true, so don't tell me about the subway."

"You're such a dodo," she said, kissing him warmly.

They went for dinner to the Casa Di Pre, an Italian restaurant on Greenwich Avenue that made the most of its limited space. All the time she had been in Vermont, Carol had been lusting for their sweetbreads cooked with Marsala. She "mmm'd" and "ohh'd" so rapturously over each mouthful that the couple at the next table – at their very elbows – stared at her. She smiled back.

Over Remy Martin and coffee, Jack said, "Did he hurt you?"

That question seemed incredibly stupid, even for Jack. She stared down at the glowing pool of her drink and asked, to gain time, "Who?"

"The man – you know – in Vermont."

"Only my self-respect," she said.

Jack realized, without knowing exactly why, that he'd asked an inappropriate question, and he displayed confusion and embarrassment as he apologized. She patted his soft hand and reassured him.

While she made soothing noises to Jack, she had a strange insight: Buster Callan had freed her. By showing her the utter irrelevancy of her partner in the act of love, he had freed her not only from Dave but also from Jack. She didn't need any particular man. She didn't need to love any particular man. No one had protected her from Buster. No one could ever protect her from the truly important things of life. She had been born alone, she had given birth alone, she would die alone. She was her own person. None of the niggling little details like an apartment or a job or a divorce had been solved, but she felt that a weight had been cast aside. She was free.

They went to Jack's apartment. They were eager to enjoy each other, and they wasted no time before going to bed. The first night, last night, had been a disaster. They had both been clumsy. Last night the thought had occurred to her that it was like trying, after a long time, to remember the skill of riding a bicycle. You were sure that it would come back to you, but in the meantime you wobbled and fell. The thought had made her laugh at just the wrong moment. But tonight it was different. She remembered the unused skill. So did he. It was perfect.

Propped on one elbow he stroked her hip, staring down at her. It was only then that she realized that they hadn't turned off the light. She averted her eyes, embarrassed.

"Did you –" if he asked her what she suspected he was going to ask her, she would scream "– ever think of going to a school or something to learn a trade, a skill?"

Her gratitude was boundless. She sighed as she stared up into his eyes. "No."

"I don't know exactly what. I mean, computer programmer, or bartender, or dealer, like in the gambling casinos. I don't know, I'm talking off the top of my head, but you could consider things like that. You could stay here while you did it, and then you could be independent."

She rolled onto her back and stared at the ceiling. "That's very sweet of you."

"I'm a sweet guy."

"I know," she said. She reached out to touch him and accidentally touched his reawakening phallus. She held it in her hand and felt it grow.

"Independence. I've been dependent on somebody else for half my life. Almost all of it, if you count my parents. I have to try my wings. See if I still have any wings."

"I know. I don't especially like it, but I understand it. And I still say you could be a topless go-go girl."

She laughed. She sat up and brushed her hair back from her face, wanting him to watch what she would do. Her hand was full. She leaned forward and sucked the fullness into her mouth.

"God, I love you," he groaned.

The phone rang. She pretended not to notice. It kept ringing. She slipped her lips away.

"Maybe you should answer that," she said.

"Why?"

"It might be important. It sounds like it's important – most people quit after ten rings."

"It's a wrong number." He rolled away from her and picked up the phone beside the bed. "Hello?"

She lit a cigarette as she watched Jack. She could see that something was very wrong.

Bleakly, she thought, maybe some girl, some very young girl, is pregnant. He rolled out of bed to sit on the edge as he listened. He made a few noises into the phone, just nervous monosyllables of agreement. He was almost shockingly tense.

"Just a minute," he said, and he held his hand over the phone as he said, "it's for you. It's your husband."

"What?" she cried, sitting up.

"Carol, this is some kind of serious emergency. I can't bullshit this guy, he's cracking up. He got my number through Cissy, that should tell you it's serious. Do you want to talk to him? I think you better."

"You're out of your fucking mind," she snapped, "you and Cissy both. She told him I was here? You've really blown it for me. Oh, Jesus Christ! Give me the goddamned phone."

She sucked hard on her cigarette as she took the phone from him. She said, "Dave?"

"Something terrible has happened, Carol," he said. "I don't know how to go about telling you this. If there were some easy way to tell you . . ."

"Dave! Will you please, please, *please* come right to the point?"

"Okay, you'll get it straight," he said, his voice suddenly cold and unfamiliar. "Mark's dead."

"No. How?"

He was silent. She strained her ear against the song

of ghostly voices on the long-distance lines. “Dave?”

“Buster’s dog. You know, the gigantic hound. I had it figured out that he’d killed Pete. That’s what the cops think, too. Now he’s taken off, him and the dog. They’re looking for him.”

“Oh, Dave. Oh, Dave.” The tears were hot on her cheeks.

“Who’s that you’re with?”

“Oh. A friend of Cissy’s. It’s a party, you know, some people. I . . .”

“Yeah. Listen.” She listened and heard nothing but the ghostly voices. Then she heard what could have been a sob. But when he spoke again, he was in control of his voice, “Mark’s funeral is tomorrow. Do you think you can tear yourself away?”

“Oh, Dave . . . please! I loved him, he was my – my son.”

“Yeah, well. I guess I’ll see you tomorrow.”

He hung up.

Chapter Nineteen

Carol had been gone a little more than two days, but she seemed like a stranger to Dave on her return. She had shared half his life, but he found that he could look at her with no special feeling at all. A pretty woman, one he probably would have given a second glance if he had chanced to see her in the street. When he tried to kiss her in greeting, she offered her cheek.

Her friends acted more like bodyguards. They clung to her side as if they were propping her up and insulating her from contact with him. They were Cissy Parker, a would-be sophisticate he had always disliked, and her latest acquisition, a pot-bellied windbag who always seemed to be doing a second-rate impression of Dylan Thomas.

Even when her brother, Paul Warren, arrived with his wife Helen, she continued to stick with her friends after the initial reunion. It was odd that it seemed like a reunion. She'd told him she would be staying with Paul in New York. Paul had done a good job of concealing his surprise and embarrassment when he'd called last night and asked to speak with Carol.

The funeral was like most of the funerals he had ever

attended, with irreconcilable family factions keeping their polite distance from each other. But why had Carol and her friends become one faction, he and Alice another? Paul and Helen fell into the role of bewildered mediators, trying to devote equal time to each side.

The minister was bland and ineffectual, but what could he expect of a minister who had never met his son? Not one word that he said registered on Dave's mind, but his presence triggered a flood of associations, memories of old words that rolled like thunder through his mind, "Thus saith the Lord, in the place where dogs licked the blood of Naboth shall dogs lick thy blood, even thine." The story of Ahab and Jezebel. "But there was none like unto Ahab, which did sell himself to work wickedness in the sight of the Lord, whom Jezebel his wife stirred up." He stole a glance at Carol, sitting beyond Alice and the man with the red beard.

Later, at the grave, she cried. Cissy comforted her. Alice squeezed his hand very hard and watched him apprehensively, and she didn't seem at all reassured when he smiled at her.

He wasn't ready to cry yet. He had things to do first.

He had looked at this churchyard once and thought that it would be a fine place to be buried some day, with cracked slates from the eighteenth century for company. Continuity and tradition weren't important to him, because he had always thought them lacking in his life. But no place was a fine place for his seventeen-year-old son to be buried. . . .

Still the minister talked, and he thought, "I will lift up mine eyes unto the hills, from whence cometh my strength." His father, who had always loved the Bible – as literature – had named him David for the putative author of that line. He should have followed the tradition and named his own son Absalom. He felt his tight control almost shatter.

He kept his eyes on the hills, far above the open grave. They were green mounds like the humps of tired animals, old, worn-out mountains that had been ground down to the bone in the last Ice Age. They didn't look very large until he compared them with the helicopter sweeping the lower slopes, which looked like a tiny dragonfly. It was probably part of the search for Buster Callan. He didn't think they would find him that way. He hoped not.

He looked back over his shoulder at Easton, the mountain where Buster used to go with his dog. No helicopters there, and he saw no movement in the cultivated patches on the slopes.

Alice led him back to the car. He heard McTeague asking where he could get a drink, heard Carol, inviting them all to the house. He wished they would all go someplace else and leave him to make his preparations, but he could think of no good way of telling them that.

At the house, Cissy exclaimed over the wood-peg floors and small-paned windows, and McTeague soon found the liquor.

"I suppose you'll be selling it now, eh?" Paul asked him.

"Selling what? The house? The thought hadn't even occurred to me."

"Well . . . the unpleasant associations, you know. And it seemed likely you could even make money on it, the way real estate prices have been soaring," Paul said.

Dave didn't want to talk about real estate prices, or anything else. "Are you staying over tonight?"

"No, I have to get back to town."

"Is Carol going back to continue staying with you?"

Paul looked acutely embarrassed, as Dave had hoped he would. "I don't know what her plans are," Paul said, edging away. "I haven't talked to her."

Carol had apparently overheard, because she came over quickly and said,. "I think I'll be staying in the city a while longer than I thought."

He nodded. This was the first time they'd spoken alone together since she'd left.

"So you're going to stay in New York, huh?"

She looked at him oddly. He realized he had sounded bored, as he indeed was. He was wasting valuable time; it would be dark in only a few hours.

"I think so. For a while," she said. "Perhaps for a few months."

When he said nothing, she said, "I'd like to get a few things together. Now that I have Cissy's car here, you know. Winter coats."

"Oh. Sure. Are those people staying over?"

"We . . . we've taken rooms at a motel."

"You, too?" His interest was only mild. "This is your house."

"I couldn't stay here . . . thinking of Mark."

He went to the kitchen for a drink, and he found McTeague. "I'm curious about this fellow," McTeague said. "Your wife told me something about his career of murder and pillage and rape."

"Murder, yes. I guess you could say he pillaged our henhouse. He didn't rape anyone."

"Oh," McTeague said, with an inflection that seemed precisely gauged to stir curiosity. But Dave's curiosity was unstirred.

The phone rang. He made a move toward it, but Carol ran in and reached it first. It seemed to be for her.

"Is he still lurking around here, do you suppose?"

"Who?" Dave asked.

"The dog person."

Dave watched Carol absent-mindedly. Someone seemed to be trying to console her, but her answers were short and noncommittal.

"Lurking," Dave repeated.

"Are you all right?" McTeague asked.

"Yes, I'll be back there as soon as possible," Carol muttered into the phone.

Dave left his drink untouched and went up to the bedroom. He undressed, hung his dark. suit and tie in the closet. He put on a pair of jeans and the Vietnam jungle boots he had bought on sale at a Third Avenue surplus store. He had read that they were the ideal boots for mountain hiking, but he hadn't yet given them a serious trial. They were light, with uppers made mostly of canvas. He had never been able to find a hiking boot that could be considered ideal.

He slumped down on the edge of the bed. Why in God's name was he thinking about boots at a time like this? Maybe he was losing his mind. He decided not. Boots were preferable to other things he could think of.

He got up to select a shirt. He reached without thinking for a red plaid, the warmest, but laughed as he dropped his hand. What he needed was a camouflage suit. Buster's heroes, the SS, had worn them in France. Maybe Buster had one. For lurking. He smiled as he thought of McTeague's nervousness. He seemed to expect Buster and the dog to come charging into the house at any moment. He wished they would.

He chose a faded green shirt and a khaki bush jacket. He went downstairs and avoided the living room and the sound of voices. The kitchen was empty now. He took his rifle from its place by the door as he started out.

He checked himself. He had no idea at all how long he would be out. He turned back into the kitchen and grabbed what came to hand: a tin of sardines, a small jar of peanut butter, a can of Argentine corned beef. He stuffed them into his pockets along with extra cigarettes and matches. As an afterthought, he rummaged through the utility drawer, found his Buck knife, and slipped it into a pocket of his jeans.

It had become a wet dry of clouds and moving vapors, hinting obliquely of rain. The mountains were veiled in luminous grays and purples. He walked quickly across the weir and through the woods to the next road. Only then did it occur to him that he should avoid roads. The police would be out in force, looking for Buster. He was carrying a rifle out of season. It would be embarrassing to be lectured and sent home.

He turned off the road and followed the course of a brook into the woods, the same brook that fed his pond. The current ran faster, tumbling over stones, as the land began tilting steadily upward.

He was soon sweating, despite the coolness of the day, and he unbelted his jacket. A fly seemed to have adopted him. It hovered, buzzing, an inch or so above his head as he moved onward. It wasn't discouraged by his efforts to swat it away.

He found the vestiges of a trail beside the brook and followed it up the mountain. At first he thought it might have been a deer trail, but it began to make regular switchbacks as the going got much steeper, indicating that it had been laid out by men – men in better condition than he was. Even with the switchbacks, his breathing became labored and his legs began to ache.

He went up through dappling sunshine and, now, intermittent showers. Up. Over rocks, over tree roots. Over boulders. He wished that he had rigged a sling for his gun and a pack for the cans of food that gouged him at every opportunity. He fought the temptation to rest by playing tricks on himself. When I reach that outcropping of rock, he would tell himself, I'll stop and rest. When he reached it, he would say, No, I meant that next one, up there.

The trail took him across the source of the brook, a

clear spring tumbling out of the rocks. He stopped and drank, looking back the way he had come. But there was no view. The mountain was too heavily forested. It would be a good choice for anyone wanting to hide from helicopters.

Now the trail played a trick on him. It started going down. He slowed his pace. Maybe he had been following a trail that went merely to the spring, not to the top of the mountain.

He began looking for alternative routes, but then the trail began going upward again.

The skyline seemed to be getting lower, indicating that the crest of the mountain was at hand. He found that hard to believe. He was sure his progress hadn't been that good. Looking at the green and gray confusion ahead of him was like doing a giant jigsaw puzzle, trying to determine whether he was looking at a patch of sky or a granite surface. He would find out, if he could endure. His lungs burned.

He found out. He reached what he thought might be the top and found nothing less than Easton before him, around him . . . above him, embracing a brimming bowlful of forest with two vast arms. He had been climbing only a ridge that screened the bulk of the mountain from view, and he felt like an ant laboring up a doorstep and boasting of its roof-climbing abilities.

And up there – way up there – he saw a line of thin, bent trees that looked like disorderly fangs, all awash with the seethe and billow of the cloud that lived on top of the mountain. Easton seemed to be foaming at the mouth, its granite jaws itching for his bones:

He sank to a seat on a mossy rock. From the valley, it had seemed like such a tame little mountain, the sort of mountain you could assemble in the privacy of your own home with a minimum of divine skills. But now he saw that the Ice Age had botched the job of grinding this one down.

He caught his breath and lit a cigarette. He was just beginning to enjoy it when he noticed the incredible amount of smoke that just one cigarette could generate. He snuffed it out, not knowing how far away the smoke might be noticed. For that matter, he didn't know how far away Buster might be. It stood to reason that he wouldn't hole up at the very top of the mountain, where the trees were thinnest. Buster could be anywhere in the vastness of the rumpled green blanket around him.

He shouldered his rifle and continued on his way. He had made an accidental discovery. The fly that had been buzzing just above his head all this time now hovered above the muzzle of the rifle, apparently attracted to the highest point on any moving creature.

He was grateful when the forest swallowed him up again. Now he could no longer see the mountain he was climbing. It had been a discouraging sight.

The condition of the trail got steadily worse. He had to climb over fallen trees and feel his way carefully through unexpected bogs. Black flies began to attack him.

At last the trail came to an abrupt end against a huge boulder, a, wall of granite seven feet high.

"Christ," he muttered, leaning his forehead against the cool rock and closing his eyes.

He pushed himself erect and studied the land around him. Maybe he had been deluding himself and had lost the trail a mile back. He saw that someone had chiseled a name in the boulder, chiseled it in impeccable Victorian script: "Hiram Ainsley, 1874." Maybe Hiram had laid out this trail, and this marked the spot where he'd been lynched and buried for his ineptitude as a trailblazer.

He found that he couldn't even smile at his own joke. The thought of burial – any burial – triggered other thoughts that he couldn't deal with.

To the left of the boulder was a sheer drop. To the right, the upward going would be far too steep. He sat on the damp ground, leaning back against the obstacle, and tried to think. Maybe he could find a log, lean it against the wall and scale it; but the odds against finding one that would be just the right size, one that he could manage alone, seemed impossible.

His whole errand seemed impossible. He studied the woods around him. The patterns made no sense to eyes accustomed to the symmetries of steel and concrete, and a deeper darkness was already beginning to congeal in the shadows. The sensible thing would be to turn back now and hope to get home before dark.

But his home was full of people he didn't want to know. Someone had apparently been urging Carol on the phone to hurry back to the motel – the same man who'd answered his call to New York last night? He wondered when that had started. It would explain a lot. It wouldn't explain why she had decided to cause as much trouble as she could before leaving.

"None like unto Ahab," he muttered aloud, "whom Jezebel his wife stirred up."

Now he was able to laugh, as he drew a ludicrous parallel between his quest and that of Melville's Ahab. Hast thou seen the white dog? He laughed harder. He found it hard to breathe, and his eyes burned. He discovered that the sounds he was making weren't at all like laughter.

He hugged his rifle against his chest and willed himself to stop sobbing. He knew that he wasn't crying over the loss of Mark or the loss of Carol, but over the loss of his own self-image as a potential man of action.

Whom could he act against? Buster? The dog? Carol? One would have made as much sense as another. That had been the point of Captain Ahab's obsession: he had chosen the whale as an arbitrary stand-in for all the pointless evil and injustice in life.

He felt once more in control of himself. It was time to abandon this idiocy, to go home and mourn his son. He stood up, bracing himself on the gun, and that was when he heard something thrashing through the underbrush toward him.

He froze for an instant, but then he dropped to one knee and worked the lever of his rifle. It didn't feel right. He worked the lever again, and no shell was ejected.

"Oh, Jesus Christ," he sighed.

"Daddy!" Alice shouted. "It's me!"

He stood up slowly, letting the rifle fall. He'd never been more glad to see anyone. In the arithmetic of despair, he'd somehow forgotten to include her in his calculations. He hugged her hard, until he realized that she was having trouble breathing, and then he stepped back.

"What are you doing up here?" she asked, studying him suspiciously.

"Playing Captain Ahab. Only I forgot my harpoons." He gestured toward the gun. "My father impressed on me that I should always unload a gun after using it, and that became a habit. But loading it in the first place never became a habit."

"I bet you forgot on purpose. I was afraid that . . ."

She didn't finish. She seemed embarrassed. It struck him that she believed he'd come up here to kill himself. He stopped to retrieve the rifle and brushed the damp mold from it with his sleeve.

"I saw you going out with the gun," she said, "so I followed you. I . . . I thought you were just great the other day, when you said how killing anything was against your deepest convictions, how you just couldn't do it. I wanted to – well, remind you, I guess."

The subject embarrassed him. "Let's go home," he said.

She smiled with relief, and he was glad that she didn't say anymore as she turned to walk ahead of him. He began thinking about Carol.

He wondered if she would expect him to finance her sojourn in New York. How long had she said? Something about "months." He should have questioned her more closely. He –

Alice screamed, and he had to make a great effort not to follow her example. Trooper blocked the path with fangs bared. Buster Callan was holding his short leash with obvious difficulty.

"What the fuck are you doing in my woods?" Buster demanded.

The crazy question evoked an unexpected chord of sympathy in Dave. Buster would have made a much better Captain Ahab than he would. Then he remembered Mark, and the sympathy vanished.

"What do you mean, *your* woods?" Dave asked, thinking it would be best to keep him talking.

"My woods. I grew up in them. Christ. Before all you goddamned tourists started overrunning the countryside, I had them all to myself. The natives got no use for them. You got no business here, coming up with your fancy women and your big cars and your money and your dope and your every goddamned thing else. You're like locusts, eating up everything. No trespassing, no hunting, no this, no that, all the time bitching for more cops and more roads and all the goddamned things you got back home in your stinking city."

"Hello, doggie," Alice said, getting down on her haunches, ignoring Buster.

Dave was on the verge of pulling her behind him, but he checked himself. Maybe she knew what she was doing. Trooper had stopped growling, anyway. He edged to the side of the trail, hoping to divide Buster's attention, but with no clear plan in mind yet.

"Coming up here with all the money in the world so's he can buy a fucking saloon and marry my woman, that's what I'm talking about," Buster said. Abruptly, frighteningly, his eyes focused on Dave as if he recognized him for the first time. He said, "You cocksucker, you killed my dog."

"You got even," Dave said. His voice broke when he added, "You killed my son."

Dave remembered the knife in his pocket, but he supposed that the gun, used as a club, would be the better weapon. Trying to seem casual, he switched his grip to hold it at port arms.

Buster's anger seemed to drain out of him. "I didn't mean for him to get hurt," he said. "Him and me, we were getting along just fine. Then he grabbed a stick, real sudden, wanting to play a game with Trooper, and then . . . I couldn't stop it. That's the truth."

"Just like Pete, huh?"

Buster's expression turned grim as he said, "Pete was on purpose."

"Hey, Trooper," Alice said softly.

Dave glanced at her. It seemed unlikely, but maybe she would be able to charm the dog. Trooper was watching her with what seemed to be idle curiosity.

"Come on down with us," Dave said. "You can't stay up on the mountain for the rest of your life."

"Fuck I can't." He laughed. "That's exactly what I'm going to do. And anybody comes up looking for me is going to wish he hadn't. I ain't going to jail for something my dumb dog did. Is that why you come here with a gun? Beat it, mister. We already done enough to each other."

"You –" Dave started to say, but then Trooper sprang, breaking Buster's slack grip on the leash. Alice went down under the hairy, muscular mass, screaming piercingly over the dog's growls.

"You stupid bastard!" Buster bellowed, flinging himself down on the dog.

He was able to wrestle the dog away from Alice. Dave saw blood on her face, but she was able to get up and dash toward him. She buried her face in his chest, impeding his efforts to help Buster.

Trooper broke from his master's grip and backed slowly away from him, growling. It took Buster a long moment to get to his feet. His left arm was bloody, and it hung at an odd angle.

"Shoot him," Buster gasped. "Shoot the son-of-a-bitch. I can't control him anymore."

Buster drew a club from his belt. When no shot was fired, he looked over his shoulder at Dave with an expression that was partly puzzled, partly contemptuous. Trooper took advantage of his momentary inattention and hit him high on the chest. Buster was flung flat on his back. He kicked at the dog and flailed his club ineffectively as Trooper shook him like a rat.

Dave pushed Alice aside and clutched the rifle by the barrel. He swung it in a high, overhand arc, leaning into the blow with all his weight. He felt bones break as the stock hit Trooper's back. The dog howled in torment.

Trooper turned toward Dave, roaring, but his hind legs were paralyzed. Dave thrust the butt of the rifle down against the thick wedge of his skull again and again. He kept doing it even after he knew the dog was dead.

He turned back to Alice. Her lip was cut, and her shoulder was gashed, but neither wound looked serious. She clutched him, sobbing against him.

"Is he dead?" she said at last.

"Both of them. You don't want to look."

She looked anyway. "He saved my life," she said.

"It was his fault your life needed saving," Dave said, tearing a strip from his shirt to bind her wound.

He sounded tougher than he felt. He found it hard

to blame Buster for anything, even now. Much of it seemed to be Carol's fault. Maybe the ultimate blame rested with his own father for filling him with nostalgia for a way of life that had never existed.

He helped Alice to her feet. She was shaken, but she could walk without his help. After a few yards he hesitated, then went back to get his rifle. He doubted that he would tell anybody what had happened. The bodies might not be discovered for a long time. Buster wouldn't have wanted it known that he'd been killed by his own dog. He would have wanted everyone to think that he and Trooper had mysteriously vanished into the secret places of the mountains that had sustained them.

www.ingramcontent.com/pod-product-compliance
Lightning Source LLC
Chambersburg PA
CBHW030815310726
48980CB00006B/504/J
* 9 7 8 1 5 8 7 1 5 5 5 6 7 *